MORTAL ENCHANTMENT

Stacey O'Neale

BY
STACEY O'NEALE

"Me!" ☺

ISBN-13: 978-1499372533
MORTAL ENCHANTMENT

Summary

In Kalin Matthew's world, elementals control the forces of nature. They are divided into four courts: air, woodland, fire, and water. At sixteen she will leave the life she's built with her mortal mother. Kalin will move to Avalon to rule with her father—the elemental king of the air court. Along the way, she's attacked by a fire court assassin and saved by Rowan, a swoon-worthy elemental with a questionable past.
Worst of all, she learns her father is missing.
To rescue him, Kalin will have to work with a judgmental council and a system of courts too busy accusing each other of deceit to actually be able to help her. But, they aren't her biggest challenge. With the Midwinter's Ball only five days away, Kalin must take over her father's duties, which includes shifting control of the elements—power Kalin has yet to realize.
As Rowan attempts to train her, a war looms between the four courts. If Kalin fails, her father will die and the courts will fall, but the betrayal she's about to uncover may cost her even more...

Cover Designer: Najla Qamber Designs

Editor: Courtney Koschel

Copy Editor: Brenda Howell

Interior formatting and design: The Eyes for Editing

This book is dedicated to all the amazing book bloggers who supported The Shadow Prince. *You'll never know how much I appreciate you! Thank you!*

By the pricking of my thumbs,
something wicked this way comes.
Macbeth Act 4, scene 1, 44–49

CHAPTER ONE

I wonder if I can get pizza in Avalon.

My life was about to change in every conceivable way, and I was thinking about my menu options. I rolled my eyes. It was time to get serious. Today was the big day. My last day in the mortal world for who knows how long. But most importantly, the last time I would see my mother. No matter how many times I begged, she refused to come with me. She insisted my dad needed time alone with me. Father/daughter bonding type stuff.

But they made that deal before I was born; spend my childhood with my mother, then once I turned sixteen, I'd move to Avalon to be with my father—the elemental king of the air court.

As far as my friends knew, I was moving to Paris. I bragged about how I'd be living in the most romantic city in the world, surrounded by cute European guys with sexy French accents. My throat tightened each time they told me how jealous they were. They had no idea how miserable I felt lying to them. Or, how I envied their freedom.

But, it wasn't all bad.

Moving to Avalon meant I could get to know my father. We get closer each time he visits my dreams, but it's not the same as having him in my physical life. Plus, and this was a big plus, I'd be a princess in the air court

1

where Dad planned to teach me to control the air element and weather magic.

A knock on my bedroom door startled me out of my thoughts.

Mom stepped inside. Most days she wore lounge t-shirts and yoga pants, but today, she had on a canary-yellow sweater and skinny jeans. Sometimes I forgot how beautiful she is. Because of our red wavy hair and fair complexion, many people mistake us for sisters. I swear, the woman never ages. I watched as her green eyes roamed the room. "Kalin, you haven't packed a thing."

Dad told me he would send additional knights to retrieve whatever I wanted, but what was the point? I doubted my collection of Pez dispensers or assorted sets of cartoon pajamas would be acceptable possessions of an elemental princess. "I wasn't sure what to bring. I mean, it's not like we've done much traveling."

I regretted the words as soon as they came out. Judging by her face, I'd say they stung a little. It wasn't her fault that we stayed in one place. Mom was always worried I might be in danger. I never understood why, especially since we'd always lived with my father's knights surrounding our house, following me everywhere. Knights who were annoying, never giving me any privacy.

"Are you nervous?" she asked.

"No." I was scared out of my mind. I didn't know what to expect. Besides my father and his knights, I had never met another elemental. I worried if they'd like me or if I would make any friends. Also, I wondered what it would be like to date an elemental. Did elementals date? These were questions I didn't feel comfortable asking my dad.

I couldn't ask Mom either. These last few weeks had been tough on her. She knew I would be leaving, but it was still hard for her to let me go. It was hard for me too. I'd never spent a day of my life without her. I wish I could understand why she wouldn't come with me. Anytime I asked about her relationship with my father she found a way to change the subject.

"What are you going to wear?"

I looked down at my black hoodie and jeans. "I guess I should wear something nice, right?"

She clasped her hands on my shoulders. "No, you should wear what you want. Your Dad will be ecstatic to see you regardless."

I had to try one last time. She might finally open up to me. I put my hands around her wrists so she couldn't escape. "I'm sure he'd like to see you too. Why won't you come with me?"

She leaned her forehead into mine. "It's complicated."

I let go of her, heading toward a pile of folded clothes on my bed. As I inserted them into my backpack, I said, "That's what you always say."

"Look, I promise you, one day we'll sit down and talk about it. But today is about you."

I grabbed the picture of us off my nightstand and placed it inside the backpack. "If you don't come to Avalon, I may never see you again."

A second later she was next to me. I turned to face her as she said, "I didn't say I'd never come. I said not right now. Your Dad has been waiting a long time for you. He deserves your full attention."

"And what about what I deserve? What I want? Did you even think about that when you both sat down and planned out my future?" I snapped.

Her eyebrows furrowed. "Kalin, are you saying you don't want to go?"

I wasn't sure. I had always known what they'd planned for me, so I never really thought about what I wanted. It wasn't until my friends started talking about their college plans that I began to resent the idea. Yet, there was a big part of me that wanted to go. "All I'm saying is it would've been nice to have a choice."

Her eyes watered. "I'm sorry, Kalin. It's just—"

"Complicated, I know." Guilt burned in my chest. The last thing I wanted was to fight with her on what could be our last day together. "Let's forget about it for now. Like you said, you will tell me when it's the right time."

She hugged me. "Exactly."

I held on, not wanting to let her go. "I'm going to miss you so much."

Sniffling, she replied, "I'm going to miss you too."

Okay, I needed to get out of here before we both broke into the ugly cry. I grabbed my backpack and slid it over my shoulder. "I'm going to go wait outside for the knights to return."

She wiped her tears with the sleeve of her sweater. "I'll wait with you."

"No, if you're there it's only going to be that much harder to leave." I hugged her again. "Goodbye, Mom. I love you so much."

"I love you too. Be careful."

I winked. "I always am."

Once I finally made it outside, the frigid midnight breeze stung my face. I slung my backpack over my shoulder and locked the backdoor. I was instructed to wait here for my father's knights to return while they checked on the travel preparations. They should have been back by now. I decided it didn't matter; I didn't need them. The forest behind my house went back about two miles, but I knew every inch. As a child, I'd spent hours wandering the dirt walkways pretending to be on a treasure hunt with my friends. I had also kissed my first boyfriend behind one of the larger oak trees on the edge of our backyard.

The weathered wooden planks of the back porch creaked with each step. I plunked down three stairs and headed straight for the dark forest. When I reached the entrance of the woodland, I turned around and took one last look at the home I grew up in. The modest brick rancher sat alone in a tucked away cul-de-sac. It was so hidden it didn't even show up on a standard GPS. I knew that had to be a selling point for Mom.

She preferred quiet, laid-back spaces to city life.

I swallowed the lump in my throat and made my way into the dim woods. The scent of wet moss filled my nostrils. I hiked at least a mile before I stopped to get my bearings. The moonlight did little to illuminate the forest floor; it had become nearly impossible to see anything more than a few feet in front of me. The overriding silence made me shiver. Reality check; I was in the middle of the woods, in the dark, with no idea how to find Dad's knights.

I should've waited—

A familiar white shimmer appeared in the distance. Even though I had spent my entire childhood in the mortal world, Dad had sent me books about the history of the elementals. The brightness I saw was a pathway— the fastest way to travel to Avalon. There were hidden paths all over the mortal world, but only elementals could see them.

Someone had just arrived.

I called out, letting them know where I was, but got no response. The light thinned until I could only see a shadow heading in my direction. Once she was a few feet in front of me, her creamy porcelain skin, slightly oversized amber eyes, and feathered wings came into view. From far away I had assumed she was one of my father's knights, but her black feathers left no question about her identity.

She was a fire elemental.

The fire court drew their power from the Earth's core, controlling everything from a volcano eruption to a simple burning match. Stories described them as both passionate and unpredictable, much like their element.

I bit the inside of my cheek to hide the excited grin trying to form. I thought about asking her to ignite a flame from her palm like the ones I'd seen in pictures, but I didn't want to come off like a moron. Minus her wings, she might have passed for a mortal in her strapless forest green tube top and dark colored jeans. The round onyx pendant embedded in silver wings around her neck was unusual, as was her twisted grin.

"Taron is a fool to leave you unattended." Her voice was calm, almost soothing, as she circled me. "It's truly a disappointment how easy this will be."

A consuming sense of unease crept from my scalp to my toes. "What's a disappointment?"

Her hand shot out, clutched my neck, and raised me off the ground. My feet dangled, and I gasped for air as I tried to make sense out of what was happening. Why would she want to attack me? Panic gagged me as I clawed feverishly at her hands, digging my fingernails into her skin.

"Are you really this helpless?" She laughed.

"Let me go," I demanded, trying to sound intimidating even though I was confused and filled with fear. I grimaced as her grip tightened.

She thrust my body into the nearest tree. Pain radiated up my spine. Had I been only mortal, she might have broken my back. Still in shock, I tried to twist away, scraping my forearm against a broken tree limb. She smirked, her hand remaining clutched around my neck. "You are in no position to order me around, girl!"

Whatever this was, it was beyond bad.

"Get away from her!" a deep voice shouted.

My attacker peered over her shoulder and her grip loosened. "Back for more, deserter?" she asked, her voice coated with venom.

Deserter?

While her attention was somewhere else, I thrust my knee into her stomach and fell to the ground. She scooped me up by my shirt, pressing my back into her chest with her fingers wrapped tightly around my neck. I drew blood when I clawed my fingernails into her hands, but she didn't even wince.

A flash of silver light whizzed by my head and my captor's grip eased. This time I was able to slip away. I stumbled. Reaching out to steady myself, I only found air and crashed onto the ground. She launched at me again and ended up straddled on top of me with one hand clasped around my windpipe. My lungs burned. Legs thrashing, I tried to wiggle free. Yet, throughout my efforts, she showed no sign of strain. Her other hand pulled shards of what I assumed was iron from her neck.

Blackness filled the rim of my vision. Frantically, I

searched the ground for a rock, but found nothing. I plunged my hand into the damp forest floor. Maybe a little dirt in her eyes would give me enough time—

He emerged out of the shadows, thrusting a large knife into her back. She arched upwards in pain, releasing me from her grasp. I rolled onto my side, gasping for air in between coughs. Hearing a struggle behind me, I glimpsed over my shoulder. The male elemental lodged another silver blade into her back before she could crawl away.

"Go!" he yelled.

Several yards away the moonlight illuminated a clearing. I got to my feet and ran toward it. By the time I reached a large row of bushes, I ached all over. *What the hell?* Since when did the fire court want me dead? I mean, she was definitely trying to kill me. In all the chaos of the last several minutes, that was obvious. But even with all the evidence in front of me, I still couldn't accept it. Why would she be after me? Before today, I'd never met a fire elemental. None of this made any sense. This had to be a mistake.

A throbbing ache drew my attention to a cut on my forearm. It was swollen and dripping blood. I tore off a piece of the bottom of my shirt, wrapping it around the wound. Peering through the leaves, I watched my attacker thrash violently on the ground. The male elemental tore the necklace from her neck, then faster than I could blink, slit her throat. Black blood spurted from her neck and onto his shirt. He jumped out of the way when her body ignited in flames and watched until all that was left of her was a pile of ash.

My rescuer stepped into the clearing. I caught his stare and slowly rose to my feet. At my measly five foot three inches, I guessed he was close to a foot taller and maybe seventeen or eighteen-years-old. His brown shaggy hair hung in waves over his eyes, the silver barbell in his eyebrow shimmered in the moonlight. A torn blue t-shirt showed off his lean, muscular build.

His appearance suggested he'd spent a lot of time in the mortal world. For every young elemental, years away from Avalon were necessary. There was no other way to mature into adulthood. The magical veil that kept Avalon hidden from the rest of the world also prevented anyone inside from aging.

Adrenaline raced through my veins. "Who was she?" My voice shook.

He glanced down at the necklace in his hand. "She was an assassin from the fire court."

My brain had officially left my body. "There has to be some kind of mistake." In all the nights Dad visited me in my dreams, he never once mentioned any tension between the air and fire courts. I thought the elementals were at peace. "She must have been after someone else."

He put the necklace in his jeans pocket and shot me a stern look. "The dead air court elementals she killed would prove otherwise."

His words burned into me like a branding iron. They died because of me. Guilt rushed over me as I imagined the loss their families would feel. "You're sure she killed them?" I knew I'd heard him correctly, but for some reason, I needed to hear it again.

"Yes. I found them only a short distance from the pathway."

If my attacker went to the pathway first, she must have been expecting me to be there. Oh God, this was getting worse by the second. "Wait. How do I know this

isn't some kind of trick? How do I know you're not working with her?" I took a few steps backwards to put some distance between us. "How do I know *you* didn't kill them?"

"The fact that you're alive is a pretty good indication that I'm not trying to kill you."

He pulled up the bottom of his shirt and wiped the black blood off his cheek. The curve of his hip was exposed, I forced myself to look away. I needed to focus, not drool over some guy who was obviously dangerous.

"What's your name?" I asked.

"Rowan."

"Were you tracking her?"

"No."

Rowan definitely wasn't big on details. "Then, what are you doing here?"

"I was in the area." He looked away and I got the feeling he was hiding something. "Taron has knights at your house. You should be there instead of scampering around in the forest."

I crossed my arms. "I wasn't *scampering*." I got impatient and stupidly decided I could find my own way to the pathway.

"Whatever you want to call it doesn't change the fact that you're alone and unprotected." The leaves rustled and Rowan tensed. "We have to get you out of here."

He looped his arm inside mine and towed me deeper into the dark forest. I had to jog to keep up. His urgency put my already amped up suspicions into epic overdrive. "Why? Where are you taking me?"

"You're not safe here. The elemental who attacked you wasn't the only one they sent. There could be others."

"This is insane!" Pulling back on my arm, I forced him to stop. "I'm not taking another step until you tell me who you are and what's going on."

"Look, this wasn't the way it was supposed to go down. I was supposed to be done, and now—" He cut himself off, emitting a low growl. "Trust me, this isn't going to make the highlight reel for me either."

His answer only confused me more. "You were done with what? You're not making any sense."

"You, I meant," he snarled. "You and your... situation."

"Wow, and up until now, I thought you were part of the welcoming party." My *situation*? What was this guy's damage? He didn't even know me. And who said I invited him to be part of my *situation* anyway?

He took a deep breath, exhaling as if he'd been defeated in a battle. "I killed two fire court assassins to protect you. Now, I have no choice. I have to return to Avalon and tell the council what happened."

Finally, Mister Personality said something I understood. The council was judge and jury to everything. The members included the four royal families and several other high-ranking elementals. I definitely wasn't convinced I could trust Rowan, but Dad was a member of the council. If that was where he planned to go, then it's exactly where I needed to be. "I'm coming with you."

"Absolutely not." He shook his head. "You need to go back to your mother's house. The knights can take you somewhere safe until I can get this mess sorted out."

I let out an exaggerated breath. "Listen, I really appreciate what you did back there—I really do, but I need to find my father. If you want to keep me safe, take me to the council."

"Last time I checked, the fire court was part of the council." He pointed over his shoulder. "I think the big pile of ash back there sent a pretty clear message."

He wasn't wrong, but I had reached my limit. "Okay, let me make this simple for you. You'll either take me to the council, or I'll scream my freakin' head off until I alert every elemental within a five mile distance." I poked my finger into his chest, which was surprisingly hard. "Do you understand me now?"

With his hands balled into fists at his sides, he said, "Fine, whatever. Walk right into danger if you insist, but don't say I didn't warn you."

He pressed his palms into the air and the blackness rippled like ocean waves. We must have been standing close to the glamour protecting the pathway. Elementals used glamour magic to change the appearance of an object or hide something from view.

A howl cried out strong enough to shake the ground, we fought to stay on our feet.

"What the hell is that?" I shrieked.

"Gabriel Hounds, which means we're officially out of time." In one swift motion, he wrapped his arms around me and hurtled us into the dark current.

CHAPTER TWO

We plunged through the glamour, hitting the ground with a *thump*. Rowan landed on his back with me on top of him, our bodies completely entwined. I gazed up briefly and he was smirking. My cheeks burned with embarrassment. I hurried to get to my feet and dusted the dirt off. A second later he stood, brushing the muck off the back of his jeans.

Less than a few feet away, a large oak tree had been split right down the middle and spread open wide enough for a doorway. Cloud-colored wind spun rapidly inside like a tornado. It must have been the pathway the air elementals had planned to use.

I tensed when his hot breath blew against my ear. "Don't be afraid," he whispered.

Oh yeah, sure.

Something tugged at my feet. The magnetic force of the hole was dragging us closer. Even though Dad had told me about the portals, I couldn't settle the cold shiver racing down my spine. Only a pure elemental could navigate through the portal. Rowan reached out for my hand as if he sensed my hesitation. The tension reduced in my shoulders and I was ready to step inside.

This was it. There was no turning back. I slid my hand inside his. The connection sent a warm sizzle up my arm as we entered the abyss.

Dad compared the experience to being sucked into a vacuum bag—he was spot on. There was nothing above, below, or on either side of us. Icy air circulated like a wind tunnel, but without any noise. We walked on a hard surface, but I had no idea what it was made of. My teeth rattled from the bitter cold. "I hope you know where you're going."

"Doubting me already?"

Of course I doubted him. I didn't feel confident about anything. I was attacked without knowing why, and then saved by someone who seemed to wish it had never happened. On top of that, air elementals are dead, and now I was traveling through a dark, freezing hole with no idea of where I was going. Who wouldn't be freaked out? "When will we get out of here?"

"It will be over any minute now," he said calmly.

A camera-like white flash snapped in front of us, and I covered my eyes with my forearm. I took a few more steps and quickly realized the cold was gone. Luke-warm air surrounded me and I let my arm fall to my side. My vision was hazy but cleared within seconds.

The moonlight illuminated the emerald green forest surrounding us in every direction. My eyes followed the primeval twisted tree trunks all the way into the sky. Dark hostile clouds hung and intermittent bolts of lightning flashed. Dampness clung to my legs as I glanced back at the ground. A faint gray mist filled the forest floor in rolling waves. Crickets chirped over the cicadas' calm song. I stood there with my hands over my mouth, unable to speak. It was breathtaking.

The pathway brought us to the edge of the woodland court forests. The Earth's natural terrain—every speck of dirt to the immense rainforest—was kept in balance by

the faeries. Of all the courts, the woodland fae seemed the most interested in the mortals, especially the arts. Painting, dancing, and music were some of their favorites. Dad said they were known to dress in high-end mortal clothes and jewelry. Compared to the air court, they were quite lavish.

A warm energy surged through me, pulling me out of my thoughts. My skin hummed as it made its way through my body. I felt stronger—alert and aware of everything around me as if I had just drank several shots of espresso. Dad told me my power would surge as soon as I entered Avalon. Within the mist surrounding the isle, I would be my most powerful. But what I was feeling now was much more than I had imagined.

During our dream visits, I would beg Dad to allow me to come to Avalon. He always rejected the idea, reminding me of his promise to Mom. They wanted me to have a 'normal mortal childhood'. Not sure how he figured I could ever be normal, but Mom did her best. As I got older, she feared my power would fully awaken, but she never tried to hide me from the mortals. There was no need—I had become an expert at blending in.

Most of my physical traits were mortal, but I had never seen anyone with bright green eyes like mine. I always thought they looked like two limes, especially since they were slightly bigger than most mortals. My hair was an odd shade of burnt red, but anyone could use hair coloring to match it.

Rowan startled me. "We need to get into the woods, it's not safe here in the open."

Before I had time to ask why, he headed in the direction of the woodland and I followed. We delved deeper into the inner sanctum of the forest. Sandy paths

I could barely see through the foggy mist went in every direction. Rowan led cautiously while we passed beautiful fruit trees. My mouth watered as their strange aromas traveled on an invisible wind straight into my nostrils: vanilla and chocolate. One particular grape vine caught my eye. It appeared ordinary except the fruit was a shimmery gold. I picked a single grape off the vine and pinched the fruit between my fingers. These fruits were used to make the wine they drank during celebrations.

About a quarter of a mile away, a luminous watery haze rose from a tiny stream. The bright liquid materialized into the form of a young woman surrounded by a glowing aura. Her inkblot-black hair hung past her waistline. As we got closer, I saw she had white henna styled markings on the edges of her pale blue eyes and cheekbones. Scaled fish fins poked out from behind her like wings. Her facial features were tiny—almost childlike—when she smiled.

A water elemental.

They controlled all the waterways of Earth and were known to be peaceful and intuitive. The fact that they only communicated with each other telepathically added to their mystery. Their real voices were like a siren's song. They could put any mortal in a trance if they wanted. Because I was a halfling, I had to be careful not to get caught up in their spells. I considered them the most dangerous of the four courts.

Her eyes bore into mine. Inside my head, I heard a woman humming a beautiful song that sounded oddly familiar. Of all the courts, I knew the least about them. Curiosity got the best of me, and before I realized it, I was heading in her direction. The angelic creature held up a wine glass as if she was offering it to me. The drink looked delicious. My mouth tasted like sandpaper. I wanted some of her refreshment.

"You cannot accept a drink from her. That water elemental is a siren." Rowan blurted, almost as if he was scolding me. "The elixir she's holding is likely enchanted. Drinking that would be like chugging ten shots of vodka, and that's if you react well."

He redirected us onto an adjacent path leading us farther from the siren. She shrugged. The light surrounding her dimmed like a sunset until there was nothing but darkness.

Once she was gone, the music silenced and so did the dehydration. I didn't want to admit Rowan was right, but he was. I stared down at my bandaged arm. "I get it. I should've been more cautious."

When I glanced up, he was staring intently at my injured hand. He must not have noticed it before. In less than a second, he stopped walking and reached for my arm. He unfastened my make-shift bandage and examined the cut. His touch made the baby hairs on the back of my neck stand.

"You should be able to mend this," he said. "It's part of your lineage."

Dad told me the healing gift was unique to our bloodline. Similar to mortals, any other elemental had to use potions and elixirs to mend themselves. I cleared my throat. "I don't know how."

"I don't have the ingredients to mix together a salve, so we're going to have to try to ignite your healing power." He cupped my free hand over my forearm, then placed his hands on top of mine. A cool breeze circled us, tickling my face. His hands were warm with hard calluses on his palms. "Close your eyes and visualize the cut mending."

"What are you going to do?" I asked.

The corner of his mouth curled into a half smile, and my legs felt like Jello. "I'm going to try to transfer some of my energy to you. That should be enough to increase your natural healing velocity."

Huh?

He closed his eyes and I closed mine. The wound sparked like tiny little prickles. I fought hard not to pull my hand back. A rush of pressure filled the incision as if water was running through it. Seconds later, I felt a tug and was sure the skin around the edges of the wound had closed back together. I opened my eyes. White light crept through the cracks of our overlapping hands. Rowan opened his eyes and the light faded. As he backed away, I peered down at my forearm. The cut had disappeared. All that was left was a fine pink line.

"How did you do that? Did my father teach you that?" Without answering, he started down another path. I sped up until my pace matched his and we walked side by side. "Yeah, sure. No need to answer my question."

"Why didn't Taron allow you to visit Avalon?" he blurted, changing the subject. "I mean, it's not like he could come to you."

No, he couldn't. Elementals were not immortal. The magical veil prevented aging as long as they remained in Avalon. The moment they left, time would gradually catch-up and they would age as they were supposed to. And since Dad was one of the oldest elementals, he surpassed his natural aging by a few centuries. Travelling into the mortal world would have killed him within weeks. "It was an arrangement he made with my mother. They wanted me to have a mortal childhood. But, he did visit with me in my dreams."

"Clever," he replied, but I wasn't sure if he was talking to himself or me. "What did he teach you about our world?"

Rowan certainly had a lot of questions for someone who didn't like answering them. "Surprisingly, nothing about you. Care to fill in the blanks?"

He cleared his throat. "Another time."

The leaves rustled in a nearby shrub. Rowan put his hand out, blocking my mid-section. We stood still, watching the bush. "It's probably just a rabbit or a squirrel," I said. Another twig snapped, tension built in my shoulders. Then I heard tiny voices. "Or, maybe not."

He reached behind his back and a leather sheath appeared with a sword inside. I stared at him curiously. Being part of a royal family meant I could usually see through an elemental glamour. If he could hide his sword from me, he came from a strong lineage. I wondered what else he was concealing under a glamour.

"Show yourself," he ordered, unleashing his weapon. He swung it once as if it was meant to be a warning.

Two little elves—walking garden ornaments was more like it—stepped into view. They didn't wear pointy hats, but they did have chubby faces and little pot bellies. I covered my grin, fighting the urge to pick them up and kiss their cute faces.

I was sure the empty expression across Rowan's face meant he was not amused. He pointed his sword at them. "Why are you following us?"

One elf waved his hand. "We mean no harm. No harm here. We saw you travel the pathway. You don't look familiar."

The other crossed his arms with his eyes squinted. "These forests belong to the woodland court after all."

Rowan took another step toward them. "We don't owe you any—"

I placed my hand on his shoulder. He stopped mid-sentence which took me by surprise. I smiled to put the elves at ease. "I'm Kalin, daughter of King Taron. I'm looking for him. He's in a council meeting somewhere in this forest."

Both elves nodded with delight. "Yes, yes! We know where to find the council meeting." They pointed farther into the distance. "Stay along this pathway and you'll—"

"I know the way." Rowan rudely announced.

The elves didn't say another word. I watched them as they disappeared into the trees.

I rolled my eyes at Rowan. "Your manners are impeccable. You must have tons of friends."

His jaw clenched. "They were wasting our time."

What a douchebag. "They were only trying to help."

He slid his sword back into its sheath, and then arched an eyebrow. "I don't remember asking for it."

Rowan was cocky, impatient, and downright infuriating. He winked and my stomach felt like a hundred dragonflies were doing summersaults. Nope, I refused to be attracted to him.

We moved quickly as we made our way through the vast forest until we came to a stop in front of a wall of hanging green vines splayed across a large boulder.

Rowan pushed the strands out of the way to reveal another glamoured entrance. He stood there motionless for a few awkward moments. Both his hands were tightly fisted. He seemed reluctant to go in there, which only put my own nerves even more on edge.

"The council meeting should've already started," he said, in a monotone voice. "I guess it's time to make our grand entrance."

My whole body tensed. I was about to meet my father. I glanced at my clothes and cringed. Covered in dirt and blood, I attempted to brush off the grime. I failed. I tried one last time to run my shaking fingers through my knotted hair. There was no fixing this disaster—I was a hot mess. I'd run out of options. Nothing left to do now but suck it up and follow him. After taking a few short, panicked breaths, I stepped inside.

I can't believe I'm walking in here like this.

The council room was a massive landing of wooden planks. Perched on top of a waterfall, the will-o'-the-wisps circled our heads like floating tea lights. Rushing water flowed beneath, and a spectacular mountain range sat in the distance. It was as if we'd stumbled into a landscape painting.

Elementals in scattered groups took up most of the space. Almost all of them had turned when we entered. They immediately ducked their heads, whispering to each other, but no one came to greet us. An uncomfortable feeling swept over me. There were so many people staring at me at one time.

My unease must have been obvious because Rowan leaned down and whispered, "Don't worry, I promise they're not staring at you."

I shook my head with total perplexity. "How do you know that?"

He didn't respond...again.

I stood on my tippy-toes to see over the crowd. At the far side of the enormous balcony, four marble chairs were strategically placed in a half moon formation. The top of each bore an etched circular symbol of the different courts: three blue circles for water, three entwined yellow twisting balls for air, burning red flames for fire, and a green tree with roots for the woodland court. I had read all about the council meetings. The elementals sitting in those chairs were the elders.

My eyebrows knit together when I didn't see Dad among them. I did make eye contact with Jarrod—his lead knight—who was sitting in the air court seat. He had been sent many times to bring me books, birthday presents, and other assorted gifts. But, why was he in Dad's place? Jarrod smiled when he noticed me. A second later, he nearly jolted out of the chair when he saw Rowan. His reaction seemed really odd. Then I watched each of the council member's eyes shifting from me to Rowan.

A united gasp from the council caused every elemental who wasn't already staring at us to turn around. The noise was sucked out of the room as if everyone stopped breathing. All I could manage was an awkward smile and a weird wave of my hand. Imagining how *stupid* I must look made my cheeks burn with embarrassment.

A woman rose from the fire court chair. Her blond hair hung loose down her back. She wore the ceremonial council robes I recognized from one of my books. I had no doubt she was the fire queen, Liana. She glared at three body-builder looking elementals in black suits standing on the adjacent side of the room. They nodded, heading toward her. Once they were by her side, she pointed her finger at Rowan. Her entire hand ignited in flame. "Escort the deserter out of these proceedings immediately!"

That was what the assassin called him. But, what did it mean?

He reached behind his head, releasing his blade from the leather sheath. As the crowd backed up, smoke rose from the skin on their forearms. The room filled with screams. One elemental caught fire. Many ran for the exit. Dad told me the weaker elementals couldn't withstand the presence of iron, but I had no idea they would actually burn.

Rowan pointed the curved blade at the fire queen. "You will answer for your crimes before this court."

The three muscular fire court elementals surrounding Liana bent down on all fours. They howled, and the wooden planks shook. My heart pounded like a drum. They were the same unmistakable cries as the ones we'd heard in the forest right before we entered the pathway.

Gabriel Hounds.

The rips from their clothing filled the air, tearing right off their backs. Black fur covered their skin while muscles bubbled from their backs and shoulders. Each one doubled in size. Thick, black claws replaced their fingers. I clasped my hand over my mouth as their faces morphed into something close to a panther. Fire burned in their ruby colored eyes. When the transformations were complete, they glared at Rowan.

My stomach twisted like a pretzel. Rowan shifted closer; his body now directly in front of mine. With his free hand, he waved them on as if welcoming the challenge.

Rowan was either the bravest person I had ever met or the most stupid.

Jarrod positioned himself between us and them. With his hands extended on each side, he said, "Enough of this!" He glanced up at the fire queen. "Call them off, Liana."

Liana smiled, eyes wild with excitement. Clearly, she was hoping for a bloody battle. Jarrod extended his arm toward the skies with his fingers spread, summoning the air element. Gusts of air whipped all around us. My hair flew into my face. Lightning sizzled in the skies while a swirling wind the size of a basketball appeared above his palm. A second later, the hounds backed up behind Liana. Rowan waited for Jarrod to calm the storm before he pointed his blade toward the ground.

Everyone who remained—especially me— took a collective exhale.

Jarrod sat back down in the chair, but Liana remained standing in defiance. I stood in the same spot, totally dumbfounded, trying to make sense of everything that had just happened. I didn't know what the hell was going on, but my list of questions grew with each passing moment. There was one question that lingered above all. One question they would answer *now*.

"Where is my father?

CHAPTER THREE

Everyone looked in my direction, but no one answered my question.

Instead, their attention returned to Liana who sneered at Rowan as if she was about to chew his face off. Her fists ignited into flames as she said, "You dare come here and make accusations against me?"

Rowan stepped closer, yanking the necklace from his pocket. With the medallion raised above his head, he faced the crowd. "The fire court ordered an attack on the daughter of the air court king. This necklace belonged to the queen's assassin." Whispers spread over the remaining group. Rowan turned, throwing the jewelry at the feet of the council members. "I demand that Liana answer for her crimes against the air court."

Jarrod picked the necklace up off the floor. The other two air court council members joined as he examined the evidence. Once they were done, Jarrod said, "It cannot be coincidence that this crime took place around the same time as Taron's disappearance."

I reeled back, stung by his words. "Wait, what? Did you say my father has disappeared?" Again, utterly ignored. It was as if I was the only one who heard my voice. I wanted to scream at the top of my lungs. I had never been so angry in my entire life.

Liana glared at Jarrod with even more fierceness.

"This is nothing more than a smear campaign against my court. The assassin in question who wears that necklace is very much alive." As she spoke, a ball of fire ignited next to her. The flame grew larger, molding into the shape of the woman who attacked me. Liana extinguished the flame coming from her hands before she reached for the necklace around the woman's neck. She removed it and flashed the medallion around the room. The charm was an exact match to the other medallion that Jarrod held. "As you can see, Malin was never sent to attack the halfling." She narrowed her gaze at Rowan and me. "They have been deceived by a glamour."

The council members and Rowan shouted. The arguments were so loud that birds flew out of nearby trees to escape what I assumed they thought was a threat. All that the council members cared about was who to blame. My arms trembled, wanting to strangle each one of them. Instead, I shook my head with disgust. I'd had enough. "Stop!" I shouted. "Your bickering isn't going to resolve anything." They were silent. "Now that I finally have your attention, I want to know what happened to my father!"

Rowan ran his fingers through his hair. Under his breath, he said, "I warned Taron that something like this would happen. He should've listened to me."

"You knew my father was missing and you didn't tell me?" He opened his mouth, but I held up my hand. Every confusing thing he had said now made sense. "That's why you didn't want to bring me here!"

Rowan rubbed his hand across the back of his neck. "No, that's not what I meant. I didn't know he was missing."

All the anger was suddenly replaced with overwhelming fear. I didn't know who I could trust. I was alone. I was in danger. Dad was gone, maybe even dead. I crossed my arms, drawing them tightly into my ribs. I tried to pull myself together while my life shattered in front of me. My throat tightened. I couldn't breathe. It was as if all the air had been sucked out of my lungs. At the same time, my mind flooded with questions. What was I supposed to do? I wouldn't even know where to start looking. Was my father attacked? What if he was hurt? "This can't be happening! I have to get out of here." My voice cracked as I willed the tears not to release. I pushed my way through the crowd and out the glamoured door. Jarrod yelled something, but I refused to stop. I ran through the forest aimlessly for what felt like miles until I collapsed near a patch of berry bushes. I pulled my knees into my chest and buried my face in my folded arms. I had never felt so alone. I wish Mom was here to help me through this.

Leaves crunched under the thump of fast-paced footsteps. I tensed when the noise ceased. Rowan leaned against a tree. "Am I always going to have to chase you through a forest? This seems to be a developing pattern."

I rubbed my hoodie sleeve across my tear stained cheeks. "This is a nightmare."

He stared blankly into the distance. "There are worse things."

"Oh, really? Thanks for all that insight," I said, scowling at him. "Was that meant to be comforting? If so, epic fail." I was in a strange world with no idea as to who I could trust or what I should do next. How could this get any worse?

There was a long silence as I watched his expression

shift from irritation to something pained. I guess he was contemplating what he was about to say. After what seemed like forever, he bent down and gently placed a hand on top of my forearm. Little goose bumps formed around the area where our skin touched. "I can't change what has happened, but I will help you find Taron." He peered over my shoulder. "Let's start by returning to the council meeting."

"Go back? You can't be serious."

He rose, and then held out his hand. "It's obvious that I don't trust the fire court, but I still have faith in the council. If you plan to rescue Taron, you'll need allies."

I stood without his assistance.

If I had to count on the council to find Dad, it was more hopeless than I had imagined. They seemed pretty worthless, but I didn't know them very well, and they have been in power for centuries. The more I thought about it, Rowan was right. I had to take any help I could get. Playing nice would be my best move at this point.

I sighed. "Okay, I get it. Let's go back."

We returned to the council area only to discover it was empty except for Jarrod. The rushing water underneath the wooden planks echoed through the surrounding trees.

Jarrod leaned against the armrest on Dad's chair. As we entered, he moved toward us. Beyond the scar running down the side of his cheek, he looked more like a politician in his yellow council robes than the leader of my father's knights. He appeared to be in his mid-to-late

thirties, but thanks to the veil, it was impossible to tell anyone's age.

Beyond the minor defect, his only distinguishable trait was his short, white-blond beard. Most elementals couldn't grow them because they remained in Avalon after they reached physical maturity. Dad told me Jarrod had visited the mortal world many times, which was why he appeared older than most. I imagined it must be hard to have to remain in Avalon when there was a huge world outside. Depending on how much I wanted to age, I would eventually have to stay within the mist as well.

He bowed. "I'm pleased to see you, Princess. My apologies for the way you were treated when you first arrived. Even after all these centuries, some in the council still look down upon halflings; even the ones with royal blood."

Is that why they ignored me? Awesome. I could add their disapproval to my growing list of problems. "I'll have to worry about that later. Right now, I need to know exactly what happened. Where were you when my father disappeared?"

He stared at the ground. "I was sent to check on the preparations for your arrival. Before I left, your father said he wanted some time by himself. That was not an unusual request. He prefers to meditate alone on the hillside surrounding the castle. When I returned, he was gone. I sent out a search party, but there were no traces of him anywhere."

My eyebrows furrowed. "You didn't go searching yourself? How could you leave him alone?"

Jarrod's tone intensified. "We followed the orders of our king." He took a deep breath, and his shoulders

visibly relaxed. "There was no reason for us to expect an attack."

I instantly regretted my behavior. Jarrod had been at my father's side my whole life. He was probably hurting as much as I was. "I'm sorry I came at you with accusations. You've been a great friend to my father and it's wrong to assume—"

Rowan let out a low growl, stepping in front of me. He was right up in Jarrod's face. "No reason to expect an attack? I can think of plenty of reasons. You should have been prepared—"

Jarrod stood, unmoving. Clearly, he was not easily intimidated. "We followed the orders of our king. That's what you do when you're loyal to your court. But I wouldn't expect *you* to understand."

Why was Rowan so angry? There had to be more to this than either of them were letting on. And what had Jarrod meant by his jab at Rowan? Forcing my way in I pushed them both, increasing the space between them. "Whatever this is between you two needs to stop. Arguing is not going to help us find my father. We need to get to the castle and see if we can find any witnesses."

There was an uncomfortable silence for some time. Rowan was the first to calm down. "You're right. Can you take—?"

"Princess, he is not a member of our court. We do not need his assistance."

Rowan squared his shoulders, glaring at Jarrod. "I am a friend to the House of Paralda. I will help Kalin find her father."

House of Paralda? It was strange to hear Dad's last name referred to as a house. Even after all of his lessons over the years, the elemental customs still felt foreign.

Jarrod reached for his sword. "Kalin is the princess of the air court. Her protection is my responsibility."

Rowan was about to say something else when I moved in between them. "Enough! I thought we'd moved past this." I locked eyes with Jarrod. "I wouldn't be alive if it were not for Rowan. I would like him to stay at the castle as my guest." He opened his mouth to speak and I put my hand on his shoulder. "My decision is final."

Jarrod huffed. He definitely was not happy. "Very well, Princess."

Rowan had a smirk on his face as he motioned toward the door. "Follow me."

When Jarrod opened the door, I was expecting to see the forest. Instead, he had used the door to create another pathway. I shuddered. "Oh, not again."

CHAPTER FOUR

It was a good thing I was not afraid of heights. Otherwise, I would've passed out. The air court's castle was embedded in the top of the highest mountain in Avalon. The colorless crystal bricks of the medieval styled palace sparkled against the moonlight. Beyond the castle walls, a hazy fog hid a very long drop to the ground. A brief ping of pain radiated from my shoulder blades. For a moment, it felt as if something was trying to push from beneath my skin. Now that I was so close to the source of our power, would I sprout wings? I hoped it was true, but the sensation quickly faded.

We trudged toward the arched passageway leading into the grassy courtyard. A massive stone fountain sat directly in the center of the quad. As we approached, thin lines of water shot into the sky in what looked like a professionally choreographed show. I spun around, counting the balconies protruding from each level. During one of our dream visits, I stood on one of those balconies next to Dad. Together, we had watched the air court elementals practice weather magic.

At the very thought of Dad, my chest ached with a mix of worry and fear.

While lost in thought, we'd been greeted by a group of air elementals. Embarrassed for not noticing them, I gave them a weak smile. They bowed in response, which

only made me more uncomfortable. No way would I ever get used to that.

Air elementals tended to marry within their own court, keeping their unique characteristics intact. Each was stunningly beautiful with their white-blond hair, lilac colored eyes, and pale yellow feathered wings. I could only imagine the scandal that took place when Dad brought Mom here. Unfortunately, neither of them ever wanted to talk about it.

Of all the courts, air was the most conservative. The men wore yellow, loose-fitting tops and matching drawstring pants. The women were a bit more stylish with yellow silk fabrics draped over them in layers. Some were strapless while others exposed only one shoulder or covered both completely. They didn't care much for heavy make-up or jewelry.

A surge of energy jolted me out of my thoughts. It raced through my veins, filling my body with a warm vibration. It was stronger than what I had felt when I first arrived in Avalon. This was intense, powerful. The skies erupted in a lightning storm. Thunder crashed loud enough to make some of the elementals duck. A bright white light flashed, and a split second later, the ground rippled with an electronic surge. A rush of heat snapped at my temple. I lost my balance and fell.

Jarrod came to my side, grabbed my arm and helped me up. "Are you all right?"

I held one hand to my forehead, trying to suppress the forming migraine. "What happened?"

"You called on the power of our element." A younger female elemental said as she approached. She had to be around my age. "This will help," she said as she rubbed a white cream on my temple. I closed my eyes and a hint of white shimmer flickered. When I opened them, the pain faded away completely. She backed up a few steps and bowed. When she rose, her bright smile made it impossible to look anywhere else.

I glanced around at the crowd watching us. They looked as surprised as I was. "It couldn't have been me. I don't know how to do that."

"I thought only King Taron could summon lightning. But since you are his only daughter, it makes sense that the power was passed on to you." She looked into the skies as the thunder continued to roll. "Without the king, it will take some time for us to calm the skies."

The elements are tied to our emotions. Something I'd felt triggered the storms, but I had no idea how to replicate it. A trained elemental could've calmed the skies. Unfortunately, Dad insisted I would be taught when I came to live with him, making me completely useless right now. Knowing there was nothing I could do, I said, "I think now would be a good time to go inside."

"You can follow me. I'm Ariel, by the way," she said, sliding the bag off my shoulder and onto hers.

The great room had air court banners hanging from every archway. The cathedral ceiling was made of stained glass, allowing the lightning storm I'd somehow created to flicker across the walls. Pale yellow candles in large golden sconces illuminated the foyer. Cream colored stones covered the walls with white marble flooring. A few scattered wooden pews lined the walkways, but beyond that, the decorations were sparse.

Our footsteps echoed the hall as we made our way along the stone floors.

I cleared my throat. Jarrod turned around as I said, "After what happened in the forest, I need a few knights to keep watch over Mom. They should stay nearby, but not close enough for her to notice." She is mortal with no way of defending herself if an elemental attacked. If something happened to her because of me, I don't know how I could forgive myself. I'd begged her more times than I could count to come with me to Avalon, but she refused. It was clear now that she should have come with me.

Jarrod pointed toward two knights who nodded back, quickly disappearing down a back corridor. "Consider it done, Princess."

We eventually stopped in front of a long wooden staircase. Jarrod put his hand on my shoulder. "You must be exhausted." He glanced at Ariel. "Please escort the princess to her room. I will get Rowan settled into one of our guest rooms."

Rowan nodded, following Jarrod down a long hallway.

Ariel motioned for me to come with her, but I raised my hand instead. "Wait a second. I can't just go to bed now. I need to know the plan. What are we doing to find my father?"

Jarrod turned to face me. "Knights are searching every inch of our territory. If he's here, they'll find him."

"What about the other territories?"

He crossed his arms. "The council members are as concerned for your father as we are. They've dispatched their own knights to search for him."

My gut told me something wasn't right. After what I saw at the council meeting, could I really trust that they were worried about finding Dad? Then I remembered what Rowan said about needing allies. "I guess that's good enough for now." Jarrod smiled at my response, but I wasn't finished. "If he isn't found by morning, I'll be going out with the next search party."

He shook his head. "That's impossible, Princess. You must prepare for the Midwinter's Ball. It's only five days away. With your father missing, there's much left to be done."

The Ball was the way the elementals celebrated the seasonal power shift. To keep the four elements in balance, each court reigned over three months of every year. The air court was about to take power, but under the circumstances, I could not imagine Dad would have wanted me to focus on the celebration. "Can't we postpone this until Dad is found?"

Jarrod rubbed his beard stubble. "If there was a way, I would've done it the moment we discovered King Taron was missing. Unfortunately, we have no choice. We can't risk the elements shifting out of balance. The Ball must happen as scheduled, even if the king is not found in time."

In all the turmoil, I had forgotten about the power display. During the seasonal power shift, the royal family ascending to power must prove they have full control of their element. During the ceremony, they are challenged by another elemental court. If they win the challenge, their elemental court will reign for the next three-month period. My neck muscles tightened as if two boulders had been placed in between my shoulder blades. "You know I haven't been trained."

"There is no one else, Princess." Jarrod explained. "Each royal house has to prove they are worthy of the power they will receive."

My hands trembled. Before anyone noticed, I shoved them in my jean pockets. Dad had performed so many power displays over the years; I wasn't sure what was expected. "What kind of *display*?"

"The fire court is currently in power which means Liana will perform the ceremony. She will likely create a large fireball, which you must extinguish using only your air court magic."

Oh, you mean the magic I don't know how to use? Perfect. "I have to put out a fireball? Like, one that's being thrown at me?" This day had been one disaster after another. My palms sweated. "That's not even possible." I searched for a way out. "I know the rules, but under the circumstances, can't you do it?"

"I cannot," he insisted. "It must be done by a member of the House of Paralda. Otherwise, you forfeit your titles."

This was all up to me and there was no way out. If Dad wasn't found, I would be the one person expected to perform the power display. The uncertainty set in and I panted as if I was about to have a panic attack. "What if I can't? What if—"

"You have to," Rowan said. "It must be done."

I laughed nervously. "No pressure there."

Rowan came to stand directly in front of me. "I'll teach you." He smelled like the cinnamon incense I used to burn in my bedroom. I leaned closer to take in more of his scent, and then abruptly stopped. *What am I doing?*

"That's not necessary." I was startled at the sound of Jarrod's voice. When the hot guy fog melted away, I turned my attention back to Jarrod—who was scowling at Rowan—like at any moment he might pounce. "She will be taught by a member of *our* court."

Even through the thick tension, Rowan's shoulders never stiffened, his jaw never hardened. Slowly, he shifted to face Jarrod. "I'm sure you can imagine why I would be the appropriate person in this matter."

Appropriate? What did he mean? Rowan wasn't part of the air court, so how could he help? What was with all the hostility between them?

Jarrod paused for a long minute. I was about to say something when he broke the silence. "Very well, you can start training in the morning."

Jarrod bowed and walked away.

Rowan's eyes met mine, and he winked before following Jarrod. They headed down the side corridor.

I was caught in a nightmare. Dad was missing, and now I had to master a power I didn't know how to control, *in only five days*. Maybe there was a chance I could find him. As far back as I could remember, Dad appeared in my dreams. If he were in trouble, he would come to me and tell me where he was. Suddenly, sleep was exactly what I wanted to do.

Someone tapped me on the shoulder. The room had emptied except for Ariel and me. She took a quick glance around. "I imagine this is all quite overwhelming."

Biggest understatement ever! "Yeah, you could say that."

She smiled. "I'm happy to help you get adjusted."

I scratched the back of my head. "You mean you want to help with the power training, too?" The upside seemed to be that everyone was willing to jump in and help. Either that, or like me, they knew this situation was a disaster in the making.

She giggled with excitement. "Oh, there's much more to being a princess than power."

CHAPTER FIVE

Ariel led me up several staircases and down a long, dimmed hallway. The winds blew out several of the candles giving the walkway a gothic hue. The only sounds were our footsteps and the occasional popping in my ears from the high elevation.

"What do you mean by, *more to being a princess than power?*" I asked, wondering what else I would be expected to do.

She turned around and smiled. "You have a prestigious position in our court and you'll be expected to act accordingly. Most likely you will need etiquette lessons so you can fit in."

"*Etiquette lessons?*"

"The way you talk, walk, eat...everything has to be perfected." I raised an eyebrow, and she continued. "Appearances are everything at court."

Then it clicked; in the eyes of the court members, I was a homely halfling—not their equal in any way. I would have to prove myself so they would help me. I hadn't been here for one full day and I was already sick of all the bureaucratic snobbery.

The thought of kissing their asses made me a bit nauseous and I frowned. Ariel must have noticed. "I know you'll pick up on it very quickly," she said confidently. "And after that's over, we get to the really fun stuff."

My tone soured. "Like what?"

"Well for starters, you can't go to a ball without a gown! You'll be so beautiful," she gushed. "We will meet with the seamstresses and they will create your dress from scratch."

Ariel continued talking, but my mind was on the events of the day. I wasn't sure what my next move should be, or who I should trust. One thing was for sure, the life I imagined with Dad was nothing close to reality. If I spent any more time thinking about this my head might explode. I desperately needed a topic change. "How did you get stuck as my tour guide anyway?"

"I volunteered. It's a great honor to work at court, and especially for you, Princess."

I came to a complete stop.

"Okay, I get this whole princess thing and wanting to be proper, but I'd really appreciate it if you called me Kalin."

I would prefer to make a friend than have a personal assistant. In my old life, I couldn't tell anyone I was a half-mortal, half-elemental princess, destined to rule the air court of Avalon. No one knew this huge part of my impending future. It was as if I was living a secret life. No matter how close I got to friends or boyfriends, I could never tell them the truth. I spent so much of my life feeling alone. I wish I could've known other elemental children. Maybe then it wouldn't have been so bad. But both my parents thought having elemental friends would make it impossible to live as a mortal.

"I can't, Princess." Ariel's eyes widened as if shocked by my request.

I shrugged. "Of course you can. I'm asking you to." She pressed her lips together. "Think of it as a royal command or whatever."

She bowed. "If that's what you prefer, Prin—"

"Kalin."

She smiled. "Of course...Kalin."

We continued down the hallway until we came to a stop in front of a wooden door. Bouquets of flowers were engraved into the door in an intricate design. Ariel turned the knob, the door opened and I gasped.

It was like walking into Barbie's dream house. The walls were adorned with hanging vines of multi-colored flowers. A king-sized bed with an island of pillows sat in the center of the room.

A large limestone fountain caught my eye. I made my way over to it and ran my fingers through the tepid water stream. I cupped my hands, leaned in, and let the water rush over my face.

When I opened my eyes, Ariel was standing next to me with a hand towel draped over her forearm. The fabric smelled of citrus. Next to the fountain, I discovered a wooden tray with a bowl of mixed tropical fruit, a glass pitcher of orange liquid, and a single glass cup.

My stomach rumbled. I couldn't remember the last time I'd eaten. I reached for an apple and happily bit into it. I had never tasted fruit so ripe. The sweetness tingled in my mouth. It must have just been picked off the tree and brought directly here. While I ate, Ariel watched with her hands clasped together. It was weird. I ate a second piece of fruit, leaving the cores on the tray.

Ariel strolled across the room, she opened another door to an adjacent room. White marble covered the walls and floors. She stepped inside and ran the water in the Jacuzzi bathtub.

I examined my bloodstained clothes. A deep soak

was exactly what I needed. Ariel poured a purple liquid inside the tub along with a handful of white rose petals. The water turned into a riot of bubbly goodness. I inhaled the sweet lavender aroma.

Ariel reached for the bottom of my shirt and I said, "I've got it from here, thanks." It was a nice gesture, but there's no way I was letting anyone undress me. That's something you do for children or really old people who can't do it for themselves.

She bowed and walked out. When the door shut behind her, I shimmied the rest of my clothes off, and then lowered myself into the heavenly fizz. While the scented steam wafted around me, I closed my eyes and allowed myself to forget about my worries for just a few precious moments.

Completely refreshed, I wrapped a cotton towel around myself and opened the bathroom door. I jumped when I realized Ariel had waited for me. "There's one last thing I wanted to show you," she said, leading me toward a huge bi-fold door. As she opened it, she squealed. The entire closet was filled with clothes and shoes.

"Where did all this come from?" I asked.

"Your father had everything brought here for you."

I rummaged through the hanging items first. Everything I picked was a designer cut twenty-eight which translated to a size six—my size. A closet designed for me? This didn't fit with the typical air court themes; they were all about simplicity and moderation. "He didn't have to go to all this trouble."

"King Taron wanted you to be comfortable. These are all the best mortal fashions," she said, pointing to the tags. "Made by all the top designers: Prada, Gucci,

Burberry, Calvin Klein, and even Versace. He's been planning for your arrival for months."

I bit my lip to hold back the tears. The design of this room with all of these beautiful things was how he saw Avalon—how he wanted me to see it. Dad tried so hard to make everything perfect for my arrival. If only things had turned out as he had planned. Pushing down the lump in my throat, I promised myself I would be brave and do whatever it took to find my father.

CHAPTER SIX

The next day I awoke to utter disappointment. Dad had not come into my dreams. Of course, he didn't have much of a chance. I doubt that I got more than two hours of sleep. Most of my night was spent tossing and turning, fearing the worst. I had run through every possible scenario that would explain his absence. Unfortunately, most of them led to conclusions I didn't think I could bear. Imagining life without my Dad made my soul ache.

I really needed a distraction before I drove myself crazy.

Outside of my window, I heard what sounded like someone sharpening kitchen knives. I leaped out of bed, poking my head out of the windowsill. Rowan was doing some serious Jackie Chan moves with a sword. A bright light flashed with each slice of his blade. He slowed long enough for me to notice the weapon had a curve at the center. The knights Dad assigned to watch over me always carried swords, but Rowan's was unlike anything I'd ever seen. Every twist of his body made me even more aware of just how dangerous he really is.

He pressed the blade of his sword into the ground. As he pulled his arm over his head for a stretch, a bead of sweat trickled down his neck and over a row of muscles on his stomach. I swallowed hard. The window's edge dug into my skin but I refused to move an inch. The tiny droplet disappeared into the waistband of his shorts. I had seen plenty of guys in gym class with their shirts off, but none of them looked like...that. He was physical perfection—a living work of art. I sat on my knees with my chin relaxed on my crossed arms, unable to look away.

"Enjoying the view?" he said, eyes suddenly on me. His chiseled face wore an overly confident grin. Clearly, he was used to being admired.

My cheeks burned.

I stood, pretending to check out the scenery. "Not much to see."

He raised an eyebrow, letting me know that he knew I was full of crap. I waited for him to call me on it, but he went right back into his workout. I took one last quick glance at his lean, defined arms, then curled around until my back was pressed up against the wall. *Snap out of it! This shouldn't be a big deal. I need to keep focused on finding Dad.* Besides, Rowan wasn't interested in me. There were no signals coming from him, so why was I even thinking about him?

Rowan was done with his workout by the time I made it outside. He was bent over a massive stone fountain. Leaning into a cascade of water, he let the liquid wash over his face and neck. The sun glistened on his back, revealing lengthy thin white scars sliced haphazardly across his shoulder blades and down toward his lower back. Besides their faint appearance, they resembled claw marks. What was he hiding?

He collected water inside his cupped hands. "You're making a habit of this," he said, curling around. As he sat on the rim of the fountain, he ran his fingers through his damp hair. "Should I pose or do you prefer watching me in action?"

I rolled my eyes, but who was I kidding? He was the definition of swoon. The worst part was, he knew that I knew it too. "Over-confident much?"

Desperately needing an aversion, I turned my attention to three female air elementals sitting on the opposite side of the fountain. They could have been triplets with their identical Botticelli faces, wheat-blond hair and ivory skin. Each wore the yellow strapless garments I had seen when I first arrived at the castle. They scooted closer together, diverting their eyes. I stepped nearer and realized they were all staring at Rowan with a very distinct expression on their faces—fear.

I scratched the back of my head while glancing back at Rowan who was busy slipping on a hunter green t-shirt. "Let's get started with your training." He slid the leather sheath over his shoulder, inserting the sword inside.

What was the deal with the scars? Why were those elementals afraid of him? "Okay, where do we go?" I asked.

He surprised me by reaching out for my hand as if he were asking me to dance. Curious, I accepted. Our fingers clasped and my skin hummed with excitement. Before I could ask another question, I was being led toward the castle gates. I tried to relax, hoping he didn't notice the goosebumps peppered across my forearm.

"Somewhere we won't be interrupted."

He loved vague answers. We made our way toward a group of air court elementals practicing what most people would assume was tai chi, but really it was weather magic. In unison, they moved from cloud hands into a single whip. The skies crackled in response. It would take their combined power to try to ease the thunderous eruptions. They each had a small portion of power compared to Dad's power. Judging by my unintended lightning display, mine will be strong as well. Assuming I ever learn to harness it.

Although the elementals seemed focused, every pair of eyes followed us as we passed. I was about to shrug it off, but then I glanced in the opposite direction. I saw several other male elementals sitting in a tight corner whispering, fingers pointed directly at us. Either Rowan hadn't noticed or simply did not care. I, on the other hand, squirmed.

"Are you really that oblivious?" I asked. He didn't respond and I squeezed his palm. "Did you happen to notice everyone staring at us?"

"I've gotten used to it." He met my gaze with a wolfish grin.

I rolled my eyes. "I don't think that's why they're staring."

He took a quick look for himself, then turned to face forward. "You sound like you have a theory. By all means, let's hear it."

"Those elementals by the fountain were staring at you—"

"Now when you say *staring*, are you including yourself in this assessment? I recall you taking in the view on several different occasions."

"For the last time, I was *not* staring at you." I was a

terrible liar. "Now, if you're done, I'd like to finish asking my question."

He let go of my hand, moving toward a white oak tree. Leaning against the trunk, he crossed his arms. "You've got my undivided attention, Princess."

My hands clenched at my sides. He could be such a cocky little prick when he wanted to be. "Fine, whatevs." I took a deep breath. "What I was saying was the elementals by the fountain looked like they were afraid of you. I want to know why." I put my hand up. "And no more elusive answers. I want the truth."

In an obvious attempt to impersonate Jack Nicholson, he replied, "You can't handle the truth."

"Oh my God. You did not just quote A Few Good Men." I was ready to strangle him.

"It's a great movie. One of the best scenes ever." He ignored my death stare and continued enjoying himself. "Okay, okay. I'll tell you what, if you admit that you *were* watching me, then I'll answer your question."

"This is ridiculous. You can't answer a simple question?" He leaned his head back against the bark, humming the final question tune from Jeopardy. My arms flailed in the air. "Yes, okay? I was watching you, but it doesn't mean anything."

"I'm sure it doesn't." He chuckled under his breath, and I wanted to jump on his back like a little spider monkey. "The truth is, I can't answer your question." He shrugged. "The elementals could be uncomfortable because they know I'm not part of your court. Most of us stick with our own kind."

He was hiding something. It had to be big, considering all the effort he was putting out. I moved closer. "No, it was more than that and you know it."

"Kalin." His tone turned serious. "I'm trying to help you, but you have to trust me."

My eyes widened. "How can you ask me to do that when you refuse to answer a simple question?"

I blinked and he was peering down at me. His face was only a few inches from mine. My heart pounded like a drummer on speed. "You ask too many questions," he said.

"Only because you avoid answering most of them." I held my ground. No way was I letting him think he could intimidate me.

He pressed him lips together, then turned and walked away. A pathway materialized a few feet in front of him. Instead of a wind tunnel, it was a swirling ring of fire. "You're kidding, right?" Then it hit me like a slap across the face. "You're a member of the fire court, aren't you?"

"Nope."

My eyebrows knitted together. "That's impossible." I pointed to the portal. "Only fire elementals use those pathways." He didn't answer. My tone sharpened. "Are you a member of the fire court, Rowan?"

He sighed. "I'm a solitary elemental." The sudden fear I felt must have been displayed across my face because he kept going with his explanation. "I was once part of the fire court, which is why I can open their portals. Are we done here?" He waved his arm toward the portal as if he was inviting me to enter.

As a solitary, he wasn't tied to any of the elemental courts. Dad once told me those kind of elementals were the most dangerous because they didn't follow any court rules. "If you're solitary, why are you helping me?"

Rowan squared his shoulders. "I owe your father a

debt. If he's alive, I will do whatever I can to find him. That's why I'm helping you." For some reason my heart ached. His explanation for being here had nothing to do with me. I immediately pushed those thoughts away. It didn't matter what his reasons were.

Rowan choosing to leave the fire court must be why Liana called him a deserter. I wanted to ask him why he left, but the burning glare he shot me signaled that our little Q and A session had ended. "Fine," I said, sliding my arm inside his. I pulled him toward the gateway while my head filled with more questions. I wanted to know about his debt to my father. Was it part of the reason he left his court? Solitary life seemed so lonely. Why had he chosen complete isolation?

The circulating flames loomed as we approached. I bit my lip as I stepped inside. The darkness was the same as the last portal. Instead of cold, the intense heat pushed against my skin. I was covered in sweat. The farther we walked, the more powerful it became. My mouth was dry and a migraine was forming at my temples. The heat penetrated in waves, as if I was walking into the sun. I shielded my arm over my face out of instinct. Rowan put his arm around me, protecting me from some of the heat. I clung to his chest, my fingers digging into his shirt.

Even with my face covered, I squinted when a bright light flashed. The temperature dropped by what seemed like a thousand degrees. I let out an exaggerated breath as I made a mental note to never, under any circumstances, travel through another fire portal.

After I was done complaining, I took in the new scenery. It was like I was standing inside a post card. Miles of empty white sand beaches surrounded us. The only noise was the intermittent sound of waves crashing into the shore. Salty air floated into my nostrils. A sparkling mist lingered over the ocean, appearing to rise into the sky. It was the magical veil hiding Avalon from the rest of the world. The misty green forest stood at least a half-mile in the distance. Under normal mortal circumstances, it would have been heavenly. But this was Avalon, the land of 'crazy-shit-can-happen-at-any-moment.'

Rowan cleared his throat.

Glancing down, I realized I was still holding on to him. I let out an odd, anxiety-filled laugh. Perfect, considering I just admitted to staring at him. I was sure he was appreciating this, which only made the moment much more cringe-worthy. I released my grip on his shirt, wishing I was invisible. And there it was, more humiliation for his enjoyment. I scrunched my face with no idea what I should say. "This is awkward."

He tried to smooth the creases that my tightly gripped fists had made on his shirt with very little success. "Try to be gentler the next time you're in the mood for a cuddle." He winked.

"Yeah," I huffed. "That's exactly what I was trying to do." Why was I letting him get me so crazed? I'd dated guys at my school. Hell, I even had a few PG-13 moments. But I had to admit, something about being with Rowan felt different. My body reacted to him. And as annoying as he was, I wanted to be close to him.

I stared at him, staring at me—waiting for a response. "You owe me some answers."

Rowan laughed. "What I *owe you* is the training I promised."

I crossed my arms. "You said you would answer my questions."

"I never told you that I would answer more questions. You need to focus on what's ahead of you, which won't be easy." He playfully tapped his fist against my shoulder. "Besides, there will be lots of time for you to fantasize about me later."

I let out a frustrated growl. "You're impossible."

"And you're wasting time."

The nerves climbed on top of one another in the pit of my stomach. Rowan was not like any of the elementals I was used to. Throughout my life, Dad had sent plenty to watch over me, but they barely spoke to me. It was like I was being guarded by the secret service. But Rowan was so relaxed, even flirty. Was he really flirting with me or was he just toying with me? Okay, I needed to stop thinking about him, like immediately.

Finding Dad was my focus. The thought that he might be somewhere hurt or dying made my chest ache. If the situation were reversed, he'd do whatever was necessary to find me. If I had any hope of rescuing him, I had to learn how to use my power. But if I couldn't find him before the Ball, I had to protect his crown. There wasn't room for failure. "You're right, let's get started."

He reached behind his back, gripping the handle of his blade and released it from its sheath. Pointing the weapon in my direction, he said, "It's called a khopesh sword. This one in particular is made of solid iron."

"Why even have iron weapons in Avalon if so many are allergic to them?" I asked.

"Knights of each court are required to carry them as a display of their power. For the most part, it keeps the other elementals from challenging the courts."

The sun's luster danced across the silver sheen. "Does that mean you're a court knight?" My eyes moved from the sword to his lips, which were now arched in the corners, then to his eyes.

"It means I'm strong enough to carry it," Rowan replied, staring at me in a way that made my knees feel like wet noodles. "I am curious to know its effects on you." Taking a few steps in my direction, he held the curved blade out horizontally, only inches from my stomach. I felt nothing. "I was right. Your mortal blood protects you from the irons' presence. In a lot of ways, it gives you the edge against a pure elemental. This knowledge could be important should you ever need to defend yourself."

My confidence had built. Feeling cocky, I slid my finger across the blade. A searing heat instantly radiated from my finger. I looked down and saw layers of charcoal colored skin had peeled away from the tip. My finger smoked like meat on a grill. "Little problem here." I wiggled my hand violently. The pain sped up my arm.

Rowan's eyes widened. "What in the world would possess you to do that?"

"Bad time for scolding, don't you think?" I shrieked.

"Try to summon your healing powers."

It was as if I had stuck my finger in a pot of boiling water. "It's too much...the burning, I can't—"

Rowan growled. Dropping his sword, he pulled me down to the water's edge. "The veil gives the water medicinal qualities. It may be able to heal your wound." He raised his eyebrows. "What are you waiting for?"

Panicked, I ran in and plunged my hand in and out of the salty coolness. When that didn't seem to be enough, I dove into the waves. Below the surface, the water twinkled with tiny white illuminations reminding me of Christmas tree lights. I reached out for one of the tiny glowing droplets. A hand connected with mine. I screamed. Bubbles erupted out of my mouth.

A siren song whispered in my head. I relaxed completely. A child-size merman with a green tail and short blue hair smiled at me. It was impossible to be afraid while staring at his cherub face. He wrapped seaweed around my finger. The burning sensation was gone in moments. Perhaps it wasn't the water with medicinal qualities after all? I reached out for him with my other hand, but he jolted as if he had heard something I hadn't. In an instant, he was gone.

My lungs burned for air. I rushed toward the surface. After a few seconds of paddling, I was back on the shore. The only ache left rested in my bruised ego.

My clothes were soaked. With my hair dripping into my face, I must have resembled a wet poodle. I climbed up on the sand to where Rowan stood shaking his head. "Do you have no sense of self-preservation?" he asked.

I had a feeling a lecture was coming. After *that* pain, I wasn't about to take any more from him. My bitch-switch flipped on. "Yeah, I'm all about the sadomasochism. I guess you figured me out."

His jaw clenched. "You need to get serious."

Oh, it was so on now. "Are you kidding me? Yeah, like I wanted to get burned. I swear, being with you is like the icing on a giant shit cake!"

Rowan headed toward the forest, mumbling something under his breath. A moment later he stopped. He made his way back to me. "You can't afford to make any mistakes, especially if it endangers your life."

It was clear I still had so much to learn. I still wasn't even sure who I could trust. Maybe Rowan, but even he refused to be completely honest with me. Again, I thought about Dad and my heart ached. I could have cried out of sheer frustration. "I'm doing the best I can. I wasn't prepared for any of this, and right now, I'm still trying to figure it all out."

"I know." He gazed into the distance, taking a long breath.

"What do you mean *you know*?"

He straightened his back. "Nevermind. Let's move on to your training."

I rolled my eyes. "Really? You're not going to tell me what you meant?"

"Nope," he replied with a cheeky grin.

Why did he insist on being so irritating? And why had I bit my bottom lip when he smiled? I needed to refocus. "Fine, time for the training."

CHAPTER SEVEN

The afternoon sun pounded down, drying my hair. My fingers wiggled through the salty knots while I silently prayed that I didn't look as bad as I imagined.

Rowan slid his leather sheath off his shoulder, placing it on the ground. Relief washed over me knowing the iron sword was farther in the distance. "Your power is linked with your emotions. If you're centered, your power will flow evenly. Without control, you'll use too much energy." He stepped closer. "The first part of your training will be finding your center. Have you ever tried to meditate?"

I snorted. "No, definitely no."

He huffed. "Sit down and close your eyes."

"How do you want me to sit?"

Grabbing my arm, he guided me to the ground. We both sat cross-legged, mirroring one another. He placed my hands on top of my knees with his hands resting on top. Heat radiated up my arms. With a soft voice, he said, "Now I want you to close your eyes and relax."

I smirked. *Oh sure, no problem.*

He tightened his grip around my hands. "I need you to take this seriously. Do you want my help?"

"Yes," I whispered.

"Then you have to trust me and do what I ask." He loosened his hold, massaging his thumbs into my palms.

Oh yeah, this was the opposite of helping. "Close your eyes," he insisted.

I relented. I had no idea why, but I desperately wanted to giggle. "Okay, my eyes are closed."

In a soothing tone, he said, "Try to turn off your mind. Listen to the sounds of the waves crashing into the shore. Focus on only that noise without thinking about anything else."

We sat silently.

I couldn't resist the temptation. I peeked out of one eye and saw that his eyes were closed. I opened both of my eyes, watching as the sunlight flickered across his face. The silver bar in his eyebrow shimmered in the light. The salty breeze blew a few stray hairs onto his cheekbones. My fingers tingled with the desire to tuck them back behind his ear.

"This isn't going to work unless you try," he said, jolting me out of my haze.

How did he always catch me watching him? Frustrated, I squirmed in the sand. Rowan was right though; I wasn't trying. Dad would expect me to make this work. If he was not found in time, I needed to be prepared to take his place. And right now, at this moment, I have to make more of an effort. I closed my eyes, focusing on the roaring waves. Random thoughts popped into my head, but I pushed them out. Starting over each time—concentrating on the ocean.

I had no idea how long we had been sitting here. "You're doing a good job," he said, breaking the silence. "Let's try taking the next step. I want you turn off the sounds you hear and only visualize yourself sitting here. Start at the top of your head and don't stop until you are at your toes. Can you see yourself?"

I tried not to break my concentration, visualizing myself sitting here. From behind, I saw my backside. I cringed, realizing my hair situation was completely out of control. Rowan was the total opposite. Even with his eyes closed, he managed to look yumtastic. I refocused on me until my body started tingling all over. It was as if my senses were alive. I was totally aware of everything around me. Each grain of sand, the ardent sun, every gust of wind—they were part of me—we were all connected somehow. What a total mind trip. I saw myself again, except this time, a soft golden yellow light swirled around my body. "Yes."

"Can you see an aura of energy around you?" he asked.

"Yes."

"That's your power when you're focused and controlled. Remaining centered will allow you to use more energy for longer periods of time." He released my hands. "As you lose control of your emotions, the color will darken. The power will become impossible to control and will drain you. Potentially even kill you."

I lost my focus completely as the panic brewed in my stomach.

"Kill me?" I shook my head. "I don't know if I'm ready for this." Dad had told me the power was part of me, but I never thought using it could weaken or kill me. The moment after I closed my eyes, I swallowed hard. The aura had darkened to a burnt orange, appearing as thick as syrup.

"You're ready. This is the only way we can unlock your power. Don't break your concentration; you've come so far already."

"All right, but if I die, I'm haunting you for eternity."

He chuckled under his breath. "I look forward to that." Although my eyes were still closed, I was sure he was grinning.

When I concentrated again, my aura was a light orange. I focused on the briny gusts of cool air blowing off the ocean. Slowly, a yellow light poked through the orange. I fixated on my slow breaths. Eventually, the color returned to a creamy yellow hue.

I opened my eyes and the warm yellow aura radiated off my skin. "It's so strong, I swear I can almost see it."

He raised his eyebrows. "Well done. You're picking this up faster than I expected."

"I have to be honest. I was really worried back there when you first started talking about the dangers, but now I get it. It feels like it's a part of me." Suddenly, I felt hopeful and grateful to Rowan. I didn't completely trust him, but I appreciated what he was doing for me. I surprised myself by pulling him into a hug.

He jolted in surprise.

I released him and stood. I could not believe I'd nearly leaped into his lap. It seemed as if I was going for the world record in mortification. Too bad invisibility cloaks aren't a real thing.

If he noticed my embarrassment, he never acknowledged it. "You managed to find your center, but do you think you can focus while distracted?"

My body tensed. "What kind of a distraction?" I wasn't ready. My instincts told me to get the hell out of here. What a jacked-up situation this was.

"I'm going to try to provoke you. I want you to stay calm. Let me know when you're ready and remember to concentrate."

This wasn't going to end well, but I didn't have a

choice. I had to do this. Conquering this would mean I was a step closer to controlling my power. I had to be brave.

I met his stare.

He wiggled his eyebrows.

With a brazen grin, he strolled behind me. I didn't turn around to see where he went. This was his test. He wanted me to flinch. I stared out into the ocean, watching the waves form. I visualized the warm yellow energy radiating from my skin.

My eyes widened.

Hot breath tickled the back of my neck while fingertips slithered slowly from my wrist to my shoulders. *Focus. Stay focused.* Every hair on my arms stood. Subconsciously, I let out a low moan. He nuzzled his face into the nape of my neck, running his nose against the back of my ear.

Spinning me around, our eyes locked.

Deep sapphire eyes penetrated into mine. There was something there that I hadn't seen before. An intensity I didn't understand. As his gaze shifted to my mouth, everything around us ceased to exist. Oh God, he was going to kiss me. My lips parted in anticipation.

Rowan leaned closer, then stopped abruptly. His face drained of emotion and he crossed his arms. "I should've known. We need to start with a smaller distraction."

No freakin' way! He was going to kiss me—I was sure of it. Nice, he tried to blame it all on me. I waved my hand in front of me, trying to play it off even though he'd won. "Oh please, that was nothing."

He smirked. "Really?"

"Yes, really."

"Then why are you blushing?"

"It's sunburn." I pointed to the sky. "In case you hadn't noticed, we have been standing on a beach in direct sunlight for hours."

"Okay," he challenged. Leaping backwards, he landed a few feet away. "Let's move on to something a bit more...physical." He tilted his head as if he was sizing me up.

My legs trembled. "What did you have in mind?"

Reaching down, he pulled his sword from its sheath. The iron weapon gleamed in the sunlight. How far was he willing to take this? A second later, he answered my question by lunging toward me with his sword aimed at my head.

No time to think.

No time to move.

An uncomfortable rush of heat ran from my shoulders to my fingertips. It pulsated like a heartbeat, urging to be released. I pointed at Rowan. The burning sensation discharged out of my hands. An explosion of wind caught him in mid-air, thrusting him backwards. He landed on his back, motionless.

"Rowan!" I shrieked. I wanted to go to him, but all of the energy had drained out of me. My muscles ached in my arms and legs. I put my hands on my hips, taking in a few slow breaths. This was what Rowan was talking about. Using my powers only for a moment left me feeling as if I had just finished an intense workout. When the weakness finally subsided, I ran to him.

I stood over him as he stared aimlessly into the sky. Was he in shock? In the bright sunlight, his eyes lightened to a pale blue. His lips were perfect—the bottom lip slightly bigger than the top. I'll bet he is a

great kisser. I dropped to my knees, brushing sand off his face and neck. A strand of sweaty wavy hair clung to his forehead. Without hesitating, I tucked it behind his ear.

Rowan swatted my hand away. "I'm fine, okay?"

As he sat up, my first thought was helping him to his feet, but he wouldn't want my assistance. Instead, I cracked my knuckles in my lap. "I'm so sorry. I don't know what happened."

"You tapped into your wind magic." He stood, shaking his head. Grains of sand flew from his hair. "That's what happened."

I rose, wiped the sand off my legs. I couldn't hold back my excitement. "It was awesome, right? I mean, I've never been able to turn on my power, and then wham! This is fantastic, what should we do now?"

I reached out for him, and he recoiled. "This seems like a good time to end the training. You did well today."

"But, Rowan—" I whined.

"You can practice your meditation on your own. For now, let's get back to the castle."

Standing with my mouth gaped open, I watched as Rowan walked toward his half-buried sword. Had I embarrassed him by knocking him down? It was an accident. Was he mad at me? I couldn't understand any of this. The whole point of this training was to unlock my power, and we did, so what was the problem? I kicked at several tan seashells with the tip of my shoe.

"Another fun-filled day in Avalon," I said to myself.

CHAPTER EIGHT

Rowan left shortly after we returned to the castle. Apparently his bruised ego needed some tending to.

I spent the rest of the afternoon in the meadow beyond the castle walls, attempting to practice meditating. Two air court knights silently watched from beneath the stone archway. I was sure they'd been sent for safety reasons, which should have helped me relax, but I couldn't focus with their eyes on me.

It didn't help that Rowan's face was the first thing popping into my mind each time I closed my eyes. The sexy curl at the corner of his mouth, the cocky way he arched his pierced eyebrow. The way his deep-set blue eyes stared into mine—breaking my concentration. With everything going on, I shouldn't be thinking of him.

Absolutely no distractions.

Needing to get centered I took in an exaggerated breath. Another image floated into my subconscious— Liana. She was furious when she saw Rowan at the council meeting. The way her arms burst into flames was frightening. What had he done to evoke so much hate from her? It had to be more than just his decision to leave the court. But even if that was her only reason, there were still more questions. Why did those air court elementals appear to be afraid of him at the fountain this morning? I put my hands over my face, growling into my palms. I could not get him out of my head.

As I practiced all afternoon, my aura burned light orange without ever returning to the yellow it had been on the beach. Meditation was not working. It was time to try something else. Maybe Rowan was wrong. Maybe I didn't need to be calm to ignite my wind power? What would it hurt to try? I focused on a mental image of my aura, envisioning myself as I pushed wind out of my palms. A jolt of heat raced up my arms as the power surged. My fingertips burned with energy, aching to be released. Flexing my fingers toward the skies, I let go of the force. The momentum of the discharge knocked me to the ground. Every joint in my body throbbed as if I was covered in bruises. I immediately regretted not listening to him.

I stared into the tangerine and purple colored skies. The day was passing into twilight. Fluffy clusters of clouds surrounded the castle. As the sun set in the skies, the mist protecting Avalon could be seen. It appeared to blanket the isle in a sparkling golden shimmer. Dad had told me how magnificent it was from this altitude, but this was the first time I'd seen it for myself. I sat for a long while as I admired its beauty, recovering from my practice.

The mountain air grew colder. I rubbed the sides of my bare arms wishing I would have worn something more than a tank top and yoga pants.

Ariel suddenly approached, out of breath. "I've been looking everywhere for you."

My eyebrows furrowed. "What's going on?"

"Didn't Rowan tell you?" she asked.

I shook my head.

For the first time since I'd met her, she looked really irritated. "He was *supposed* to send you to me so we can get *you* dressed for dinner."

Dinner? "That's news to me. Who will be there?"

Ariel's face lit up. "The entire air court council, of course. They will be here in less than an hour. We need to move quickly."

She waved her arm and I followed. I still wasn't fully recovered as I struggled to keep up with her. We sprinted across the grassy courtyard toward the castle entrance. Once inside, we marched up the stairways until we were back in my bedroom when she all but threw me into the bathroom. Clearly, I wasn't the only one who thought I needed refreshing. I turned the faucet on in the tub and prepared for a quick bath.

Once I'd finished, I walked out with a towel wrapped around my chest. Ariel had a dress laid across my bed. I strolled over to the mirror and held it against my body. This was more than a dress; it was a golden yellow ball gown. The tiered, skinny-strapped, floor length gown had a jeweled black belt around the waist. It was something I would expect Princess Catherine to wear while dining with the Queen of England.

"The dress goes on last," Ariel said, getting my attention. "First, we have to do something with your hair."

Twirling a few wet strands around my finger, I said, "I usually let it air dry. That's about the only way to contain the curl."

She made her way behind me, twisting my hair into a loose bun. "Which is exactly why you'll be wearing it up."

I raised an eyebrow. "You say that like I have no choice."

"You always have a choice, but this is part of my job." She let the bottom portion of my hair hang down my back, maneuvering the top into another style. "You'll end up loving what I do, I promise."

"So actually, I don't have a choice." I teased.

Ariel smiled. "Not really."

I sat in a chair, watching her through a vanity mirror. She primped and curled my hair into all kinds of formal designs that I'd only seen in prom magazines. For a moment, I pretended I was back in my old life preparing for a school dance. Mom would have been part of every step from picking out the dress to perfecting the hairstyle. A knot settled in my throat and I swallowed hard.

It had only been one day and I already missed her so much. I thought about contacting her a thousand times, but how could I tell her Dad was missing? She would insist on coming here. I refused to put her in any danger just because I missed her. I couldn't allow myself to get depressed. Right now, Dad needed my help. I had to stay focused on finding him and learning to control my power. Otherwise, we would lose everything. "Is all this really necessary?" I asked. "It's just a dinner, right?"

"Yes," she said, patting my shoulder. "It is imperative that they see you as the princess you are."

It only took a moment to remember their distaste when I spoke at the council meeting. To them, I was nothing more than what they saw—a halfling, covered in muck and blood. The dinner was important. I had to show them I was one of them. I had to earn their trust so they would help me. But how?

When Ariel was done, the hair at the crown of my head had been pinned up with tiny white flowers sewn within. Loose curls hung down my back. Without a doubt, this was the most stylish my do had ever been.

As I reached for one of the strands, my chair spun around. "Not so fast," Ariel said. "Let the artist work."

Ruffling through a silver pouch, she pulled out brushes of every size and lined them on a small glass table. In no time at all, she had applied glittering make-up on each eyelid and cheek. With the tip of her finger, she slid a gloss over my lips. The grin across her face gave me the impression she was pleased with her efforts.

"What do they typically discuss during these dinners?" I asked.

"I can't say for sure. Only members of the royal family, the council, and high ranking knights are invited." Ariel bit her lip. "I would guess you can learn quite a bit about the inner workings of the court by attending."

If she was right, this dinner might provide all the answers I had been looking for. And at the very least, I could get to know some of these council members. Perhaps even make some alliances of my own. My chest burst with hope.

Ariel turned my chair to face the mirror. I suddenly felt like I was on one of those make-over shows. Hardly recognizing myself, I stepped closer to my reflection. My brain couldn't accept what I was seeing. This was about as polished as I could get.

And for once in my life, I actually looked like a princess.

"I can't believe it's me."

Ariel's expression turned serious. "Not so fast, Cinderella. You're not ready for the Ball just yet."

"What could be left?" I asked.

"Princess training; the crash-course version." She pulled back on my shoulders to straighten my posture.

"When you enter the dining hall, look straight ahead. Never lower your eyes. You must exude confidence."

"Anything else?" I didn't mean to sound rude. After all, she had done nothing but go out of her way to try to help me. Truly, she was the first and the only elemental friend I had. Rowan didn't count. I had no idea what the hell he was.

My impatience for the situation got the best of me. None of this should have been necessary. The council should be on my side because I'm their princess. Whether they liked me or not was irrelevant. Helping me meant getting their king back, unless that wasn't what they really wanted. I pursed my lips. Could Dad have been taken without help from someone within our court? Is there a traitor amongst our council? I quickly shrugged off the thoughts. No, it wasn't possible. My irritation toward their behavior made me suspect them without any proof.

Ariel cleared her throat. "It's important that you wait until your chair is pulled out before you sit. Once seated, thank everyone for joining you for the evening." She glanced out the window, letting out a defeated breath. "Unfortunately, we don't have enough time to go over food etiquette." Her tone turned harsh, I wondered if she was internally cursing Rowan for not telling me about the dinner. "When it's time to eat, follow what everyone else is doing. No large bites. No talking with your mouth full."

"This is lame. Are you going to tell me to keep my elbows off the table next?" I crossed my arms. "If you really want to help me, figure out how I can get the council on 'Team Kalin'."

"It may seem *lame*, but proper manners will help

them see who you really are. This may not be power training, but it's just as important." She turned away, obviously offended.

Tension spread across my shoulder blades. What she was teaching me was important. My mind drifted back to my training with Rowan. He'd also tried to keep me focused. I lowered my head; I had acted childish. Why was I standing in my own way while they tried to help me? "I'm sorry, Ariel. I appreciate what you're trying to do for me and everything you have already done."

She helped me step into the dress, throwing the towel to the side. "I know you do. I honestly don't understand how you're handling all this so well. I think I would've run away by now, or at the very least, went into a full-on breakdown."

We both broke into a laugh. I reached out, pulling her into a hug. I'd waited my whole life for a friend like her. Someone who knew all about me. Someone I could be completely honest with. If it weren't for her and Rowan, I definitely would've lost it by now.

"All right now, I don't want you smudging my masterpiece." She fluffed the bottom of my dress. "Now, get down there and make me proud."

CHAPTER NINE

Golden doors were held open by two male palace guards, both dressed in satin yellow robes. I stood beneath the entryway, holding in a gasp of breath. The vaulted ceiling was made of glass. Intricate wood cuttings covered every wall while large white pillars framed every corner. A musician sat in the farthest corner playing a harp. Servants rushed in and out of the room with glasses of amber colored wine and plates of various appetizers.

The silver crown Ariel insisted I wear felt awkward. As I made my way toward the table, I ran through everything she'd said only moments ago. I needed to exude confidence, so I tilted my head slightly, relaxing my face. A smile didn't seem appropriate.

Members of the air council were seated around a massive wooden rectangular table in the center of the room. Each wore lavish yellow robes and dresses. A large plant with multi-colored flowers, bright berries, and fruits covered most of the table. I came to stand next to the only empty seat, which happened to be at the head of the table.

The music stopped abruptly and each person stood. "Welcome, Princess," Jarrod said, bowing. Every other member gave a respectful nod, and I did the same in return. They stared at me for an uncomfortable minute until I realized they were all waiting for me to sit. One of the female servants helped to bundle my gown and I plopped into the chair. Immediately everyone seemed to sit in unison.

No one spoke. My hands shook in my lap. I cracked my knuckles—a nasty habit I picked up to hide my nerves. Sweat pearled on the nape of my neck as the temperature of the room rose. I had to do something to break the tension, but what? Normally, I would have said a joke or something sarcastic, but would a princess do the same?

"We are very pleased to have you in Avalon. To Kalin, heir to the House of Paralda." Jarrod raised his wine glass filled with the amber liquid. "Welcome home, Princess."

Welcome home? The cold shoulder reception from the council wasn't anything resembling a long-awaited homecoming. They made me feel more like a tightly lodged pebble, stuck in the crevice of a shoe. I wished more than anything that Dad was by my side. I had a feeling his presence would wipe those nasty looks right off their faces. An ache swelled in my chest as I worried over his continued absence.

The council members held out their glasses, but no one glanced in my direction. They reacted as if they were being forced. "Welcome home," they said, their voices sounding monotone.

I wanted to give them a proper one finger salute, but the gesture wouldn't win me any allies. Tipping my wine glass forward, I said, "Thank you." I focused on the wine swirling inside the glass, thinking about what Rowan had said. Was this one of the drinks he had warned me about? Would it be like chugging ten shots of vodka? Rather than take my chances, I took one tiny sip.

A council member with incredibly long white-blond hair turned to Jarrod. "Any word from the search party?"

Jarrod cleared his throat. "They haven't found anything near the area where we believe he was taken. Not a single clue was left at the scene. They have searched through every inch of our territory and found nothing."

This was exactly as I'd feared. They were no closer to finding him than they were the day I arrived. And instead of helping them, I was preparing for the Ball, where I was sure to embarrass myself. I tried to hide the panic brewing in my chest. "What about the other courts?" I asked. "What have they found?"

A few of the council members let out an irritated gasp. It seemed even the sound of my voice annoyed them. "We must be cautious when requesting information from the other courts," Jarrod said.

"Why?" My voice was sharper than I had planned.

A pixie-cut blond woman with purple jewels in her hair turned to me with eyes squinted. She seemed pained to make direct eye contact. "This is a delicate situation we're in and protocol must be followed. We cannot simply ask the courts for their results. It would be taken as an insult. We must trust that they will tell us when they have new information."

Her snotty tone was enough to earn her my bitch stare. It took every ounce of my patience not to give it to her. "So, the plan is to wait on them for information?" I shook my head. "We have to come up with something better. Perhaps, if I could go to the council meeting and speak to the leaders of the other courts directly? Maybe—"

"Princess Kalin," Jarrod interrupted, a softness to his tone. "We empathize with your urgency for results, but you have to understand, we have our own methods for getting these matters resolved."

What I understood more than anything was that my father would not be found anytime soon and the system I was working within was only making the situation direr. There had to be some way for me to move the search along. I had to find a way into those council meetings, but how? Learning my power and preparing for the Ball took up the entire day. I didn't expect either to let up anytime soon.

Rowan had said he wasn't part of my court. Because of that freedom, he probably knew Avalon better than anyone. Maybe I could persuade him to help me? My muscles weakened. It had been a while since I'd eaten. The servants had already left with the appetizers before I sat down. I reached out, plucking a few of the berries from the massive centerpiece. I popped them into my mouth.

A large piece of the bitter fruit lodged in my throat. I gagged, unable to breathe. In a panic, I grabbed the tablecloth. The tug on the fabric was enough to knock the wine glasses over, spilling on several council members. They collectively shrieked. I tried to stand. Jarrod raced around the table, positioning behind me to perform the Heimlich maneuver. After a few seconds, I spit the berry onto the table.

"They're not edible, Princess. Only meant for decoration."

In between my heavy panting, I heard curses and laughter. I wished I could sink into the floor. This evening had been a total disaster in every way. I had to get out of here. Without another word, I headed for the door while Jarrod pursued me.

"You don't have to leave," Jarrod said. "We can go back."

"No," I croaked.

"Then at least let me escort you to your room."

Since he was still following me, I didn't appear to have a choice. I kept a pretty fast pace as I headed to my bedroom. Behind me, I heard something that sounded like a chuckle. I stopped. When I turned, I saw it was Jarrod laughing. My chest filled with anger. I pointed behind him. "You think all that back there was funny?"

Jarrod pressed his fist on his mouth, clearing his throat. "My apologies, Princess. I wasn't laughing at you. It just occurred to me that your mother had a very similar experience the first time she had dinner with the council."

A ping of surprise jolted through me. It was hard to imagine Mom in Avalon, and at the very least, meeting with the council. But since Dad couldn't spend time in the mortal world without aging rapidly, it made sense that he must have brought her here. Unfortunately, Mom never spoke of her time in Avalon—she refused to say much of anything about Dad.

As Dad's second in command, Jarrod must have known Mom very well. He likely knew more about their relationship than I did. "What were they like when they were here together?" His eyebrows furrowed. "My parents, I mean. Before I was born."

He shrugged. "I would say they were very happy. King Taron doted on her constantly. She appeared to appreciate all of his attention."

We resumed our stroll toward my room. "What went wrong?"

He shook his head. "I don't believe that's a question I'm qualified to answer."

I raised an eyebrow. "I'm just asking your opinion, that's all."

He lowered his head. "Princess—"

I punched him playfully on his shoulder. "You know, I could command you to answer."

His face turned stern. "That's not fair."

"It never is." I smiled, cheekily. "Now, what's the answer?"

He huffed. "It took a turn for the worse after you were born. Your mother was not aware that King Taron could not leave Avalon. When he told her that you would be raised by mortals, she refused to leave you. Taron insisted she stay with him. In the end, they made their arrangement, but that's all I know."

The arrangement was that I would spend my first sixteen years living as a mortal, then return to Avalon to rule. But that didn't explain why Mom wouldn't come with me. She never dated anyone after Dad, which made me believe she still loved him. I was convinced there was more to their story. I hoped when Dad returned, he would fill in the blanks for me.

It must have been so difficult for her. My grandparents died when she was a teenager and she had no siblings. She was completely alone. Once I reached my door, I turned and gave Jarrod an awkward smile. "Well...thanks for, you know." I shrugged.

Jarrod placed his hand on my shoulder. "The next council dinner will fare better. I'm sure of it."

I nodded, shutting the door behind me. It really couldn't get much worse.

As soon as he was gone, my thoughts returned to my night from hell. I growled in frustration. Acid burned in my stomach while wetness lined my bottom eyelids. Those stuck-up council members didn't deserve my

tears. They should have been working with me, but instead, it was all a hot mess. Staring at my reflection in the mirror, I roughly wiped my palms over my eyes. Makeup smeared across my cheeks. I glanced down at my dress which represented everything I hated about them and their whole stupid society.

The gown needed to come off—now.

I ripped the straps off first. The sensation gave me a sense of freedom. I couldn't stop. Buttons and strings flew through the air while I tugged and ripped my way out. The last seam released. What was left of the dress fell to the floor.

"Why didn't you prepare me for this?" I screamed into the empty air as if Dad could hear me somehow.

Burning liquid raced up my throat. I made a beeline for the bathroom. Clutching the sides of my royal toilet, I emptied my stomach. There was not much in there. Once the dry gagging ceased, I pressed my cheek against the cool bathroom floor. As my eyes closed, I let the tears flow freely.

A knock at my bedroom door rattled me from sleep. Again, no dream visits from Dad. I wished I could control my power. If I could, I would be able to contact him. But who was I kidding? I wasn't even sure if his ability would pass to me since I was only half-elemental. I couldn't ask any of the council. If they knew I didn't possess the power, they would see it as a weakness.

My back ached from lying on the floor for who knows how long. Grumbling, I pushed onto my elbows, managing to stand. I nearly fell over when I saw my reflection in the mirror; swollen red eyes with smeared make-up. Wild hair sticking up in every direction.

I could have auditioned for a zombie role on The Walking Dead. I turned on the faucet, wetting a hand towel. I rubbed it over my face. Another series of knocks reminded me that someone waited at the door. I threw on a robe I found hanging from a rod. The tiny garment barely covered my thighs but it was the only piece of clothing I spotted. Twisting my hair into a clip, I made my way to the door.

Of all the people who could have stood here, why did it have to be Rowan? He took a step backward, giving me a once over. "Wow," he said, laughing. "I thought you were having dinner with a bunch of boring council members?"

Mortified, I left him standing at the door while I dashed into the bathroom.

"Had I known it was *that* kind of party, I would've crashed it." He must have come inside my room, because after the door shut, his boots thumped across the floor.

I scrambled around my bathroom searching for anything I could change into. Folded beneath the vanity mirror, I found my Jelly Belly pajamas. Someone must have sent knights to my house to retrieve my belongings. Rainbow colored beans peppered the drawstring pants. I slipped them on along with a button-down long sleeve shirt.

I can't go out there wearing this.

Mom had bought me those PJ's back in middle school. The outfit came as a free gift when she purchased a huge container of every jelly bean they made. We spent one afternoon mixing all the different kinds, making up our own flavors. After eating the entire container, we were both sick for days. It was one of my favorite memories with her. "What do you want, Rowan?"

"I wanted to make sure you are all right." His voice was close enough that he must have been right outside the door.

"I'm fine," I griped, trying without success to get a hair pick through my knotted hair. "You can go now."

"If you're *fine*, then why do you look like an extra in some B-rated horror movie?"

"That's hilarious, really." I managed to get my hair somewhat sensible and dabbed a little concealer under my eyes. This was about as good as it was going to get. No matter how hard he laughed at my clothing, I promised I wouldn't let it bother me. I needed to keep the conversation short. Get him out of my room as soon as possible.

I opened the door with tension in my shoulders as if he'd already reacted.

Rowan was lying on my bed with his arms crossed behind his head. His leather boots were on the floor, his shirt was pulled up a tiny bit exposing a slice of his toned stomach.

I will not be attracted to him. Nope, I refuse.

"I didn't mean it that way. I only came here—" He took his time admiring my silly outfit. I was expecting him to laugh, but instead, he smiled proudly. It was cute.

"Yeah, I know. You wanted to make sure I'm okay, and I am, so you can return to wherever you came from."

"Ouch." He rolled onto his side, checking me out again. "I gotta say, I was really feeling the robe, but

there's something about a girl in cartoon pajamas that does it for me."

My cheeks burned as I desperately tried to hide how much his words excited me. I made my way over to the bedroom door, tapping my hand on the handle. "Did I mention everything is fine? You can leave."

He smirked and sat up. "Simmer down, Jelly Bean."

The pajamas were a mistake. "Don't call me—"

"Easy now." He held up his hands in defeat as he stood. "I didn't mean to piss you off. I came here because I heard what happened."

Again, sickness bloomed in my stomach. I guess the news had spread throughout the castle. No surprise I was the big joke. "Which part did you find the most entertaining? The part where they barely acknowledged my existence or when I choked on a table decoration?"

"I knew they wouldn't be easy on you. The elders disapprove of halflings." He watched me for a second as if weighing his next response. "But they are still our best ally in the search for your father. It's important you keep trying. You can win them over. It will take some time."

I pressed my back against the door, letting out a frustrated growl. "Time is the one thing I don't have."

Rowan put his hands in his jean pockets, strolling over to me. The color of his eyes had cooled to deep blue. It would have been very easy to get lost in them. Leaning against the wall next to me, our shoulders nearly touched. I did my best to ignore the way my body ached to get even closer. "I do believe the council will help us find Taron," he said "They need him as much as you do."

I was taking my anger out on the wrong person. "I'm sorry for acting so bitchy when you got here. I'm just really worried, and I dumped it on you."

The corner of his mouth curled. It made me feel all squishy inside. "No apology needed. Your Dad's missing, and the council isn't helping. I get it."

I shifted my stance until I faced him. He mirrored my movement. Our eyes locked, sending a tingle down my spine. Tonight, his scent was a mix of warm cinnamon and soap. "You told me Dad had helped you out of a bad situation. What happened?"

A chilly breeze blew through the curtains dimming the candlelight. I rubbed the sides of my arms.

His face was all shadows, which gave him a fearsome hue. For an uncomfortable few moments he didn't say a word. It was obvious he didn't want to tell me. I was about to change the subject when he spoke. "I was brought to this castle badly injured and Taron used his power to heal me. He could've let me die if he wanted, but he decided to save me. Afterwards, he offered me asylum in his territory."

The scars on his back flashed in my mind. I wanted to ask more questions about the injury and the asylum, but the fact that he had opened up made me afraid he would shut me out if I pushed too hard. "It's a good thing Dad got to you in time."

Rowan made his way over to the windowsill. As he stared out into the darkness, he said, "If it wasn't for Marcus, he never would have."

A member of the air court? "Who's Marcus?"

He paused for another long moment, then shifted his body in my direction. "My best friend."

I couldn't help being caught off guard by the mention of his *best friend*. Rowan said he was a solitary. Didn't that mean he was alone? "Where is Marcus now?"

In an instant, his face lost all emotion. Share time was clearly over. "It's been a long night for you," he said

softly. "I'll let you get some rest." Just as he was about to walk out the door, he glanced over his shoulder. "Goodnight, Jelly Bean."

CHAPTER TEN

I totally sucked during our next training session at the secluded beach. After many annoying hours of meditation, I could not hold onto my calm, yellow aura. The problems with the council and the impending Ball weighed heavily on my mind. I tried to concentrate on the salty air gently wafting around us. Failed. The waves crashing against the white sand shore. Nope. No matter what I focused on, my thoughts lingered back to my troubles.

Rowan decided that we needed to change gears. He wanted me to practice my air court powers. It was no surprise that I couldn't ignite my wind magic. My body tensed with each attempt. A trail of sweat surfaced across my brow. Each time I failed, Rowan's lips pressed together into a thin line as if he was holding back what he wanted to say. After many frustrating tries, I let go of my concentration and wiped the moisture away with the back of my hand.

Rowan circled me while rubbing his hand across his cheek. "Maybe I'm going about this all wrong."

"What do you mean?" I asked, crossing my arms across my chest.

"Keeping calm has always been the way I control my power, but yesterday, you were afraid. Your power awakened when you felt threatened."

If he was planning to come after me with his sword, I wasn't having any of that. "Fine, I'll pretend I'm scared and see what happens."

He flicked his wrist. In an instant, a baseball-sized ball of blue fire materialized. The damn thing was floating in a circular motion about an inch or so above his open palm. "No, your fear has to be real for this to work."

Holy Shit! "I thought you said you were a solitary?"

He raised his eyebrows. "I am."

I crossed my arms to hide the fear shaking my limbs. "Okay, then how are you still able to ignite fire?"

"Some solitaries do lose their elemental powers all together." He shot me one of his infamous smirks. "But my family has been part of the fire court for centuries. My connection to the element is stronger than most."

No wonder the other elementals feared him. Not only could he kill with his crazy sword fighting skills, but he could also turn someone into a freakin' pile of ash. "Well, fire boy, I'm glad to see you've kept your mojo. Now, please tell me what you're planning to do with that thing?"

He cupped both hands beneath the flame, and it doubled in size. "Provoke your anger."

"Keep talking, you're bound to piss me off in no time." Would he burn me to prove a point? He edged toward me. I backed up. "Stay away from me, Rowan." I tried to sound stern, but my voice shook.

"Stop me. Push me away like you did yesterday. Find your center and focus." He took another step closer. "Come on, Jelly Bean. I know you can."

My eyes squinted. "I told you not to—"

"Do something about it." He waved the ball of flame

so close to my head that I felt the sting against my ear. "What's the matter, Princess? Am I too much for you to handle?" He bounced the ball between his hands. "I'm not surprised. I wasn't expecting much from you anyway."

Anger boiled in my chest. "You weren't, huh?" If he wanted to irritate me, mission accomplished. My power surged from my shoulders down to the tips of my fingers. "I'll show him what I can handle," I mumbled under my breath. Pointing at Rowan, I released a surge of energy from my fingertips. The sheer power knocked us both backwards and I landed on my back in the sand. The gravel scraped against my skin. I tried to stand, but my arms and legs were as limp as a wet rag.

He grabbed me under my arms, pulling me to my feet. "You're still using too much energy because you're not keeping your emotions under control. This is why the meditation is important. To master your power, you have to learn to quiet your mind."

I wiggled my arms, trying to shake off the numbness. "Sure, Yoda. I'll get right on that."

Rowan rolled his eyes. "Be serious."

I made a disgusted face, but I had to admit, I did lose my focus. "I'm trying, but I feel like I'm never going to be able to make this work. Like I'm doomed to fail on an epic level."

"That's not going to happen," he insisted.

"You can't predict—"

"We need to keep working." He pointed to three pink seashells lying on top of a sand mound. "I want you to move them. Push them off the hill."

They couldn't have weighed much more than a feather, but my hands ached from the last time I tried to use my power. I didn't want to try, but there was a determined look on Rowan's face. He wasn't backing down so I relented. "All right, fine." I closed my eyes, envisioning the three shells flying off the hill. I held out my hands, pointing in their direction. I felt a spark like a static shock.

"Open your eyes," he whispered, sending a warm tingle down the side of my neck.

My eyes flickered open. I had to hold back from squealing and jumping. The mound was empty. The shells were lying close to the water's edge. I had finally managed to do something right. "I did it!"

"Yes, you did," he said, eyes searching the beach. "Now, let's go for something a bit bigger."

I twirled around, noticing a boulder bigger than both of us in the distance. "I think I found something." I pointed to it.

"I was thinking something about the size of a basketball. You're not ready for something that big."

"Oh, come on." I gave him a wicked smile. "We're only days away from the Ball, which means we've got to speed these lessons up."

He scratched the back of his head. "This isn't a good idea."

I wanted to do this. I had to do this. "Afraid I'm going to show you up?"

"No, I—"

I didn't wait for more of his disapproval. Closing my eyes, I took a few deep breaths. My mind was dark except for a faint yellow blinking light. I had never seen the yellow so pale, and I wondered if I had used too much power. My arms were sore, numb at my fingertips. I thought about taking a break for a second. But if I had used too much power it wouldn't work, so what's the big deal in trying? I pictured the boulder, imagining it rolling toward the ocean. I reached my hands out as if I was attempting to roll it.

An odd feeling settled between my shoulder blades. It was a pressure like I had pulled a muscle. A massive muscle. I ignored it, keeping my focus on the boulder. Something changed suddenly. I was spinning except I stood still. Dizzy, I fell to my knees. I was weakening. It was like my energy was being sucked right out of me.

With arms wrapped around my stomach, I grimaced. My eyelids were heavy and I collapsed completely. The sand scratched against the side of my cheek.

"Kalin!" Rowan shouted.

Everything went black.

When I opened my eyes, my head was nestled in his arms. "Are you okay?" he asked, his eyes were wild and panicked.

I rubbed the side of my head and tried to sit up. "What happened?"

Instead of helping, he pulled me into his chest with his arms wrapped around me. His embrace was like a winter coat during a snowstorm. I was safe and protected. If only I could stay here forever. I didn't want it to end. "You passed out for a few seconds."

"Did I move it?" I whispered.

Shaking his head, he replied, "It wobbled. That doesn't sound like much, but it was. You should have never attempted something like that. You're lucky it didn't drain you completely. A power drain could put you in a coma or kill you."

There wasn't an inch of my body that wasn't aching

with pain. "I may not be in a coma, but I feel like I was run over by a herd of elephants."

He chuckled, releasing his hold slightly. My head settled into the crook of his arm. Tenderly, he brushed the sand off the side of my face. His dark blue eyes bore into mine with a fervor I didn't understand. I had to remind myself to breathe. Even after the muck was removed, he continued touching me. First, he followed my jawline with the tip of his finger. Then, he slowly traced my mouth. I swallowed hard when he licked his lips. His eyelids were at half-mast as he leaned in closer. I was overwhelmed with excitement. He was finally going to kiss me. My nerves caused me to tense up for only a second, but it was enough to ignite a change in him. It was like watching someone wake up from a daydream. Before I knew it, he was moving me into a sitting position.

Dammit!

He was all business with his tone. "I warned you this might happen, but it seems to be impossible for you follow to my instructions."

"I was listening." I barely grated out.

"Of course you were." He moved farther away, staring out into the distance. The rejection was like being punched in the gut. "This seems like a good time to end our practice for the day."

No, he couldn't leave now. "Really, I'm fine. We should keep going." I stood on my own. Another wave of weakness flowed through me.

Then, everything went black again.

CHAPTER ELEVEN

I stood in a darkened room lit by a few candles in silver metal sconces. When I took a step forward, a few round, multi-colored poker chips scattered across the hardwood floor. My foot slipped and I glanced down. An ace of spades playing card was stuck on the bottom of my shoe. I picked it off, flicking it away. The scent of burnt ash wafted into my nostrils.

An urgency buzzed through my limbs that I couldn't explain. I had the sense that something I desperately wanted was close.

"Is anyone here?" I yelled.

There was no response. Nothing about this place looked familiar. My nerves shifted into overdrive. I was about to turn around and go the other way when I heard a tiny whimper. I took a few steps forward, noticing something large crouched beneath a sliver of light. My adrenaline pumped as I went to my knees. Whoever it was had their face covered by a dirty wool blanket. Their body was curled into a ball. I reached my hand down. "I won't hurt you."

"Kalin?" He winced.

The cover pulled back. My father's lilac eyes stared up at mine. His face was covered in dirt with dried blood stained across his cheek. "Dad? What happened?" I attempted to pull him up, but he only groaned. "We've got to get you out of here."

"There's no time. We only have moments." He reached for my arm. His frightened expression nearly brought me to tears. "Do not trust them," he choked out. "They aren't who they seem."

My mind raced along with my accelerated heartbeat. "Who, Dad? Please tell me." The room started to change shape around us. Everything turned gray. The walls melted. I looked down at Dad who was fading away. I tightened my grip of his arm. "What's going on?"

"They've found me."

I opened my eyes, screaming. "Dad!"

"It's me." Ariel stood beside my bed, patting a wet cloth over my brow. "You passed out while you were training. Rowan brought you here."

"You don't understand." I sat up, still shaking from what I'd just seen. "I saw my father. He was weak and a prisoner somewhere."

"Kalin, it had to be a nightmare." Ariel rubbed the side of my arm. "You were drained of all your power. There's no way he came to you. If he had, it would have killed you."

Why didn't Ariel believe me? Panting and covered in sweat, I shifted my gaze around the room. The scent of ash had been replaced with a warm caramel. I was in my bedroom inside the air court castle. The skies outside my window were dark. Had I slept through the day? The vision seemed to only last a few seconds.

"No, it was real," I insisted, putting my bare feet on the cool floor. When I tried to stand, I couldn't hold my own weight, landing back on the bed. "I have to find him. He's in danger."

Ariel sat down next to me. "You can't go looking for him like this. Now is the time to rest. Jarrod sent out more knights to search for him." She put an arm around my shoulders. "I have faith they will find him."

The vision was real. Dad was in trouble, risking everything to warn me. He said *they aren't who they seem,* so there must be at least two elementals working together. Unfortunately, I had no idea who '*they*' were. It could be any one. Ariel smiled, trying to lift my spirits. I wished I could believe so blindly, but the council had done nothing to make me feel they could help. No, I was going to have to rescue my father alone. First, I needed to check out the area where he was last seen before he was taken. There had to be clues that they missed somewhere.

"You're right, I should just get some sleep." I hated lying to her, but there was no other way to get her to leave.

"Of course." Ariel collected the wet rag and water basin. "I'll be back in the morning." Her eyes brightened. "Tomorrow, we'll get fitted for our ball gowns."

I tried to muster a smile. "Can't wait."

She clearly wasn't fooled by my faux excitement. "I promise, I'll make it as quick and painless as possible."

"That's more like it." I winked.

She playfully rolled her eyes, closing the door behind her.

The moment the door creaked shut, I stood. The dizziness wasn't as bad as before. Maybe I just needed some fresh air. I got dressed into a pair of dark jeans, slipping a black t-shirt over my head. I glanced around the room. "What's a girl gotta do to get a weapon around here?"

By some miracle, I managed to slip out of the castle without being seen. Unfortunately, I wasn't as lucky in the artillery department. Two palace guards secured the room. There was no question that one of them would have followed me or reported me to Jarrod since he commanded the knights. I didn't want him involved in any way. Who knows? Any of his knights could've been one of the elementals Dad was referring to.

Once I reached the stone archway, the mountaintop winds whipped all around. The cool nighttime air made me shiver. Jarrod hadn't been specific when he spoke about Dad's last known location. He did say he was meditating on the hillside of the mountain. Since most of the peak was capped with snow, he could have only meant the southern side where I'd gone after my first practice with Rowan.

I dug my hands into my pockets, heading toward the grassy hillside. Gusts of air blew my hair in every direction. I pulled it up into a ponytail to keep it out of my face. The distance to the hillside was short, but all I had for light was the incandescent moon. With most of the landscape in shadow, why had I not thought about bringing something to illuminate my way? I rolled my eyes at myself as I kept trudging forward.

The terrain descended the farther I went. The dizziness I had felt earlier gave me the illusion I was falling. I was running on pure adrenaline, with only the worry for Dad pushing me forward. Dark clouds surrounded the mountain, I could barely see the thick elm tree a few yards in front of me. I made my way in that direction. Every other tree on the mountain was part of the forest and at least a mile away. I guessed that the single tree existing in the middle of a barren field would be a good place to meditate.

Once I reached the tree, I leaned against it. The sturdiness helped me regain my balance. I closed my eyes, exhaling deeply. A warm sensation came up behind me. I jolted.

"What are you doing out here?" A stern voice asked.

CHAPTER TWELVE

Rowan stood behind me with a swirling ball of hazy blue fire floating above his open palm. The flickering light bounced off the tight muscles of his bare chest. A pair of drawstring black cotton pants hung loosely around his hips. He ran his other hand through his scruffy hair giving him a just-rolled-out-of-bed look. I would have classified him as smexy if it weren't for his pissed off expression.

"How did you know I was out here?" I asked, squinting. Forget about the whole passing out mess. I was annoyed by his second almost-kiss during our last training. He was the king of mixed signals.

He clenched his fist, diminishing the ball of fire into nothing. "Sometimes, I wonder if you have a death wish."

Naturally, he didn't answer my question. Big surprise. "I have no idea what you're talking about." Chilled air whipped between us. I wrapped my arms around my mid-section. I couldn't help noticing the lack of goosebumps on his skin. I guess being born into the fire court meant never being cold.

Rowan let out a growl, pressing his fists into the tree at my shoulders. I was locked into an immovable position. There was no squeezing out of this one. With my arms pressing against my sides, he leaned in. Our

faces were so close, his breath tickled my cheek. "Have you forgotten I've saved you once already? There are dangerous creatures out here. What was so important that you came here alone *and* in the middle of the night?"

Suddenly, the stupidly of what I'd done registered in my head. This was exactly how Dad was captured. And his power surpassed mine a thousand times over. I would be defenseless.

My cheeks burned from embarrassment. Luckily, the shadows hid my reaction. Rowan was right, of course, but I couldn't let him know. "I can handle myself or have *you* forgotten *you* have been training me?"

His stare poured into me as if he was searching for the right words. Somehow, in the silence, I sensed there was something he was trying to hide. It wasn't until he pulled away, I realized I'd stopped breathing.

"You still haven't answered my question," he said.

I raised my eyebrows. "Neither have you."

Rowan paced like a caged animal. "You're infuriating."

"Oh. My. God." I threw my hands up in the air. "You've got to be kidding me. You're the king of avoidance."

After several awkward moments without a response, he relaxed his shoulders. "I couldn't sleep. I was walking down the hall when I saw you slip outside and I followed you to see where you were going." He raised his pierced eyebrow. "Happy now?"

Not really. I was too shocked that he answered one of my questions to enjoy the small victory. "I came out here looking for clues that the knights might've missed." I rubbed my hand across the bark, swallowing hard. "This is where I believe Dad disappeared."

"Oh, I get it." He leaned against the tree trunk. "Still, come get me the next time you decide to play investigator."

Smartass. "Whatevs."

"It's pretty spectacular up here," he announced, totally out of nowhere. Then, he sat down and crossed his legs in front of him as he leaned back on his hands. "I can see why Taron likes it so much."

Was Rowan initiating a casual conversation? After my initial shock settled in, I took the cue and sat beside him. "This place feels the most familiar to me. I mean, I guess I feel like this is where I'm meant to be, you know?"

"Don't you miss your Mom?" His voice was soft, almost comforting.

I pulled my knees up into my chest. "I miss her a lot, but it's complicated." I missed my friends and the life I'd built there. I missed Mom most of all. But with everything going on, I was glad she wasn't here. Avalon was not the peaceful place I had imagined it to be. And since she was mortal, she was safer where she was. "What about you? Where are your parents?"

He picked up a rock, casually throwing it into the cloudy abyss. "Dead."

Great call, Kalin. He's sure to go running any minute now. I was about to put my hand on his shoulder, but I pulled it back at the last second. "I'm sorry."

Instead of making eye contact, he continued tossing rocks. "It's fine. I've made peace with it."

I had to keep going while he was being so open. "What were they like? Your parents."

"I never knew my Dad. He died around the time I was born."

Rowan's jaw clenched and unclenched before he answered each question. He was obviously uncomfortable, but this could be my only opportunity to get to know him. I had to keep pushing. "What about your Mom?"

He looked at me, surprised. "You really don't know, do you?"

My lack of knowledge seemed boundless at this point. "I guess not."

"My mother was powerful and feared. She wasn't much of a parent to us." He took a long pause. "It's not something I like to talk about."

"By us, you must mean—?"

The corner of his mouth twitched. "I had two adopted siblings, but both are dead."

His whole family was dead? Okay, he had some serious family drama. It certainly explained why he was a solitary, but not why he turned down Dad's offer to be part of the air court. What was his deal? "How did they die?"

He turned to face me, smirking. "It's complicated."

I couldn't rebut after I had said the same thing. "Aren't all families?"

"Some more than others."

CHAPTER THIRTEEN

I didn't sleep much that night. Instead, I leaned against the windowsill watching the sun rise with my bed comforter wrapped around my shoulders. My body was exhausted from the power surge, yet each time I closed my eyes, I saw one image; Dad lying bloody and beaten on a cold floor. An icy chink settled in my chest. I tightened my grip of the blanket.

His warning echoed in my head. Who were the people he mentioned? He said they weren't as they seemed, so I must have already met them. At least one of them had to be in the air court. There was no way he could have been captured without help from someone on the inside. Someone who would pretend to be my ally. I rested my head on top of my folded arms. Dad could have also meant Rowan. As much as I didn't want to consider it, I had to. He had secrets, was a former member of the fire court, and all of his family was mysteriously dead. No matter what Liana said at the council meeting, a member of the fire court had attacked me the day Dad was kidnapped.

No, it couldn't be Rowan.

He was the one who saved me, bringing me to Avalon safely. He offered to train me—and even though I was sucking at it—I would be lost without him. But why was he so guarded? And, who gave him the scars on his back? Why did Liana seem to hate him so much? Too many questions left unanswered. The guy was the definition of complicated and secretive.

I rubbed the crusties from the corners of my eyes, longing to stay in my room all day. A hard knock shook me from my thoughts. I turned my head as Ariel entered my room carrying a cup of orange juice and some kind of pastry. Her white-blond curls bounced as she made her way to me.

She gave me the once over, then her smile dropped. "What happened? You look like death. Not that death is a person, but if it was, it would be you right now."

I wanted to tell her the truth, but what could I say? She didn't believe my vision was real. And, as much as I hated to admit it, she was also a suspect. Dad said someone I knew couldn't be trusted. I trusted Ariel, but I would be a fool if I didn't at least consider the possibility. "Nothing happened. I didn't sleep, that's all." I yawned.

"Sleep later." She sat the food down on the nearby table. Next thing I knew, she'd tucked her forearms inside mine and was helping me stand. "We've got to be to the seamstress in ten minutes."

Oh, no. I'd forgotten all about the dress fitting. With everything going on, this was the last thing I wanted to do. I may have let out a little whimper. However, Ariel wasn't having any of it. She meant business this morning, dragging me around the room like a ragdoll. I didn't fight her when she scooted me into the bathroom to brush my teeth or when she tugged me toward my closet to pick out clothes, but I reached my limit when she tried to get me undressed. Finally, I shooed her away, and she gave me some space.

Yup, I was going with her whether I wanted to or not.

Ariel led us to a room with walls lined with spools of fabric piled on top of one another. A large rectangular table sat in the middle of the room filled with sewing machines, needles, threads of every color, and multiple pairs of scissors.

Five seamstresses greeted us. I had to blink twice before I could believe what I was seeing. Their skin appeared to be made of tree bark with hair made of thin green vines hanging wavy down their backs like dreadlocks. All wore matching white silky tops and skirts made of long woven flower stems. Like soldiers, they stood silent in a straight line, staring forward. Each held a sewing kit and spare pieces of cloth tucked under their arms.

Ariel stepped onto one of the two tree stumps in the corner of the room, instructing the glam squad. "I expect something exceptional. For the princess, a one shoulder or strapless gown would be best. Something with an A-line shape would look nice on her." She played with a loose curl in her hair. "My gown should be strapless and have a matching shawl. I prefer an empire waist. Has the fabric arrived?"

They bowed in unison while the one standing the farthest away reached down, picking up an enormous amount of cloth wrapped around a long spool. I made my way over to her, running my fingers across the material. It was the softest silk I'd ever touched. Never had I seen the shade of shimmering yellow that Ariel had chosen for me. The small piece of 'girlie' I had inside of me giggled.

"It's amazing, isn't it? It took the manufacturers in Paris six months to make. It's one-of-a-kind." Ariel sighed, filled with pleasure. "It's perfect for the Ball." She held out her hand, helping me onto the stump next to the one she stood on.

"What about your dress?" I asked.

Ariel pointed to a spool of sparkly lavender fabric. "Purple is my favorite color."

I smiled. "It's gorgeous."

She kept her eyes on the material as one of the seamstresses carried it over. "I know, right?"

Two creatures appeared in front of each of us. They measured, poked, and prodded while Ariel stood quietly humming to herself. I tried not to stare, although I desperately wanted to run my hand over their skin. They were a different breed of elemental. Something I'd never seen in the books or during my dream visits with Dad.

The questions I had about their surface texture were answered as their fingers grazed against my bare skin— definitely tree bark. They had to be fae from the woodland court. Each time they nicked me, tiny bloody scratches appeared. I winced. My subtle complaints did not seem to matter since they continued to work without any acknowledgment. The one taking my measurements called out to the others in a language I didn't understand. Whatever she said sent them over to the spool of material. They started cutting.

"What are they?" I whispered to Ariel.

She glanced at the seamstresses then smiled at me. "I'm so sorry, Kalin. Sometimes I forget you're still new to Avalon. We call their species of fae, brownies. They're the best dressmakers in all of Avalon."

The one standing closest to me smiled proudly. For a brief moment our gazes locked and I admired her bright moss colored eyes. "Do you understand their language?"

Ariel adjusted the top of her dress material so less cleavage showed. "No, only the faerie king and queen of the woodland court can translate. They never speak our language, but I have no doubt they could if they wanted to."

I watched to see if anyone would respond, but none did. It was clear they weren't revealing anything to us today.

After hours of standing silently, I could barely keep my eyes open. My mostly sleepless night had caught up with me. All I could think about was passing out. I actually fell asleep a few times. Startled by the sharp pain of a sewing needle in my ribs was not cool. These brownies were ruthless.

When I finally looked down to check out their progress, I nearly went into shock.

The spool of fabric I had admired only a few short hours ago had been cut and sewn into a full-length yellow silk gown. I swayed from one side to the other, still not believing what I was seeing. To be sure, I ran my fingers down the asymmetrical one shoulder strap, then across the glittering diamond star-burst accentuating my bust. The gown was amazing. The most beautiful I had ever seen.

"I would guess by the look on your face that you're pleased," Ariel said.

I couldn't take my eyes off my new hotness. "This dress is insane. I can't believe how quickly they put this together."

I glanced over at Ariel as she admired her own strapless gown with matching shawl. It was exactly as she'd requested. "I told you. They are the best in all of Avalon." She winked at the brownie, who smiled back, proudly.

I yawned. "I'm sorry. I'm just so exhausted."

"I know what you need." Ariel clapped her hands. One of the guards stepped inside the room. "Please bring the princess a glass of sunrise wine."

"Is that like a Red Bull?"

"Sunrise wine is infused with herbs which will give you a natural pick-me-up. I drink it when I need a boost. You'll feel much better in a matter of minutes."

The guard returned carrying two wine glasses on a gold tray. The liquid was amber, similar to the other wine I drank at the dinner with the council, except this was much darker. He brought the first glass to me. I took a sip. It tasted like sparkling honey. "This tastes amazing. Thank you."

I continued sipping my drink while the woodland faeries moved around the room. Although they never spoke, they worked in harmony as if each one knew what the other was doing at all times. It reminded me of a dance. Ariel was talking about the details of the Ball, but I wasn't listening. Instead, I watched the woodland faeries as their pace slowly sped up. They moved quickly around the room. Their sewing increased to a rapid speed. The needles moved up and down faster than a sewing machine. I tried to keep up, but they were too fast. My eyes blurred. I was suddenly dizzy. The room spun. Ariel was still talking, but the words came out as if I'd pressed the fast forward button on a TV remote control.

"Stop it! I can't understand you," I screamed at her, closing my eyes and squeezing my fingers into tight fists. My fingernails dug into my palms. Something shattered and shouting echoed in my head. I couldn't make out the individual voices. Too much spinning. I tasted metal on my tongue. My stomach churned. Sweat dripped down my back. My knees wobbled. I couldn't balance myself.

"What's happening?" Ariel shrieked.

There was a burning sensation coming from my mid-section. It was as if someone had thrown boiling water on me. The pain increased with each passing second. "My skin is on fire. Get this dress off of me."

The brownies raced over to help. We pulled and tugged at the fabric until the dress was off. I gasped. Rashes covered my entire body. The brownies were panicked, speaking to one another in their language.

The seamstresses took the dress away. They stood in a circle checking out the fabric spool while I stood in my underwear and high heels with my arms over my exposed chest. Ariel quickly put a silk robe on me. The cloth did very little to comfort me. "What would cause me to break out in these rashes?" I asked, shaking. "What is that fabric made of?"

"It is hypo-allergenic," Ariel insisted.

One of the brownies let out a pained scream. The yellow spool she was holding fell to the floor. The palm of her hand had been burned. Ice ran down my spine. "Could the fabric have been poisoned?"

A few of the brownies nodded, agreeing.

"Guards!" Ariel called. "Take this fabric to Jarrod. He'll want to lead the investigation. Tell him we need to know who had access to this material."

The guard wrapped a coat around the fabric so he didn't touch it. As he walked out the door, I realized my hand was bleeding. In all the craziness, I'd shattered my wine glass. My palm was covered in cuts filled with shards of glass and blood. My dizziness return, and I sat on the ground. "Can someone help me?"

"Oh no!" Ariel said, covering her mouth. "Do we have a medical kit in here?"

Two of the brownies rushed over carrying a bag made of twigs. Inside, they had containers of different liquids and creams. They used their sewing needles to remove the glass from my hand. Without any kind of pain reliever, I could feel every scrape. It made me want to vomit. While they bandaged me up, Dad's warning rang in my head. Someone I trusted would betray me.

I glared at Ariel as an echo thrummed in my ears. "You're trying to sabotage me."

The floor around me was covered with sharp pieces of glass and droplets of wine. A few woodland faeries cleaned up around us while Ariel stood in front of me with a stunned look. "What are you saying?" she asked, eyes welling with tears.

"You're the one Dad told me about. The one who would betray me. You insisted on this dress fitting. You picked out the fabric."

"Kalin, please. The poison is still in your system. We need to get you to the—"

I put my hand up, stopping her mid-sentence. "I don't have any proof, but I will find some. And when I do, there will be no mercy for you."

Ariel backed up, her eyes as wide as tennis balls.

I couldn't trust any of these elementals to help me find Dad. He was right. *I* had to find him. Avalon was an island, not a country. There were only so many places he could be, right? I shook my head, trying to think clearly. He was in the fire court. I was sure of it. I would find him without any of their help, and when I brought him back, I would make sure they were all punished for their actions.

I stood, taking a few wobbled steps before I was able to balance.

Ariel reached out. "Princess Kalin, please let us help you."

"No! I don't need your help—any of you." I pulled my injured hand from the woodland seamstresses' grip. "I'll find him myself."

Her shoulders sunk. "What are you saying?"

I squinted at Ariel. "I'm out of here...and don't even think about following me, traitor." I headed out the door, slamming my shoulder into the wall as I rounded the hallway corner. She continued to shout my name, but I kept going until her voice was little more than a whisper.

I'm coming, Dad!

CHAPTER FOURTEEN

I was going in circles as I tried to get to the artillery room. Every hallway appeared identical to the next. The poison blurred my vision. I rubbed my eyes, but when I stared at the walls, the painted murals remained distorted. All the colors seemed to blend together. I finally gave up, deciding to search for another alternative. The winding cement staircase a few feet in front of me offered a new option. I took it. After at least ten minutes of trudging down what seemed like hundreds of steps, my legs burned from exhaustion. Thanks to my unexpected exercise session, the effects of the poison had nearly diminished. The musty air filled my nostrils as I stumbled all the way to the lowest level of the air court castle.

I stood on the final landing, glancing down at my bandage. Blood seeped through the white bandage. It would have been smarter to let them finish before running out.

I thought about Ariel and covered my hands over my face.

Once again, I had managed to embarrass myself. Why had I yelled at Ariel? How could I blame her for the poisoned dress? Even worse, how could I have accused her of having anything to do with Dad's disappearance? I had no proof that she had betrayed me. She looked terrified, flinching as my hateful words spewed out. It was the reaction of someone who had no idea what was going on. My stomach twisted in knots as her voice calling my name echoed in my mind.

Somehow, I had to find a way to earn her forgiveness.

A worn, unmarked wooden door stood in front of me. Senses intact, there was no way to rationalize storming into fire court territory to search for Dad. The war it would cause was too risky without solid proof. Running away from Ariel was the most stupid thing I could have done. I had to go back.

I stared blankly at the basement entryway. Guilt and regret reeled wildly in my mind. I could comprehend two facts; I was an idiot and I had no idea how to get back to where Ariel was. With nothing to lose, I twisted the rusted bronze handle, pulling until the door opened with a screech. I headed inside.

The windowless walkway echoed the clink of my heels against the cobblestone floor. Dimmed candles in rusted sconces barely kept the area lit. A cold draft pushed against me, I shivered as goosebumps rose from my forearms. If Dad had a dungeon, I was sure this was it. I fully expected to find jail cells with prisoners inside.

I sprinted forward, hoping to find a staircase. All I could think about was getting back upstairs and apologizing to Ariel and the woodland faeries. They had worked so hard on my dress and I had ruined everything. Not to mention, they had also cleaned and bandaged my hand. Yeah, calling myself a jerk doesn't even begin to describe how badly I had behaved. After my latest ginormous failure, my thoughts lingered back to Dad.

I needed help.

I had to trust someone.

Rowan felt strongly that I could trust the council. It was time I called for an emergency meeting to discuss the dream vision. Regardless of my personal feeling, we need to work together if we were going to find Dad. I wasn't sure how to arrange a meeting, so for that, I needed Jarrod—my only ally on the council.

Near the end of the pathway a bright light shone through the bottom of a sealed door. Shadows beneath flickered from movement inside. Why would anyone want to be down here in such a dank space? Were there really prisoners in the castle? Excluding the snobby council members, the air elementals were so peaceful and kind. This repugnant area didn't fit anything I knew about them.

Curiosity got the best of me, I quietly approached until I stood directly in front of it. Deep toned male voices came from inside. There were at least two from what I could tell. I touched the metal door and the skin on the tip of my finger seared—it was made of iron. There could only be two reasons an elemental would be in there; imprisonment, or someone who went to great lengths to stay hidden.

Something deep in my core screamed foul.

I needed to know who was inside of there, but they couldn't discover me. Putting my ear against the door would cause serious pain. Scrambling to my knees, then down onto my stomach, the cobblestone floor cooled my cheek as I tried to peer under the door.

Through the small opening, I could only peek with one eye. Inside was a tattered cream colored sofa with rips in the seams and a cushioned brown chair on the opposite side of the room. A thin layer of dirt covered the rock flooring, which gave me the impression that this place wasn't used very often. As far as the elementals were concerned, I couldn't make out anything above their waists. One had a pair of expensive looking leather dress shoes that matched an equally expensive black suit pants. The other wore suede sandals and yellow pants. One of them was part of the air court. But who was the other swanky dressed elemental?

They spoke in hushed whispers. A least that was all I could hear thanks to the thick iron door. I repositioned until my ear was closest to the opening.

"We can't afford any mistakes. Everything must go exactly as we planned." The man with expensive shoes paced, so I guessed he was the one talking. A ping of fear slithered down my spine when I realized one of the elementals sounded like Rowan. Could it really be him? The voices were too muffled to be positive. If it was him, why would he be down here discussing council issues? I answered my own question when I decided it was because he was doing something he didn't want them to know about.

"I have no doubt it will. The council is exactly where I want them. They suspect nothing," said the air elemental.

The one who sounded like Rowan stopped pacing. "And the princess?"

Anger burned in my chest. They were discussing me. I was sure of it. The air elemental plopped lazily into the cushioned chair. "She isn't a concern."

Not a concern? My teeth clenched.

What was he planning and why was Rowan alone with this air elemental? In my gut, I knew this was tied

to Dad. I tried to move closer to the door. A tinge of pain surged the tip of my ear. I winced.

In a split second, the stranger moved to stand directly in front of the male who might be Rowan. "Do not underestimate her." His tone was intense and guttural.

"Relax," he replied, letting out an uneasy chuckle. "By the time we reach the Ball, all will be in place and you'll get everything you want."

"Not what I want," Rowan said. "It's getting back what belongs to me and my family."

I wanted to blast through the door and begin my own line of questioning. Of course, if it was Rowan, I would strangle him first for his betrayal. These two had to be the ones Dad warned me about. Rage bloomed in my belly as tears welled in my eyes. It all made sense in an instant. Of course it was him. This mystery air elemental made sure Dad was alone, he probably had the advantage of surprise. He would have known how to take Dad down, and he could've gotten someone out of the castle easily. No one would have suspected someone from the inside, but who was he? His voice was too low for me to identify.

I second-guessed myself almost immediately.

I could not be sure. The voice sounded like Rowan, but I had spent the bulk of my time with him. If he was responsible for all of this, why would he have taken the time to train me? We were secluded on a beach for hours at a time. He could have killed me a dozen times if he wanted to. Really, the voice I heard could have been any male I decided. And the only basis for my theory was a muffled voice. I wished there was a way to know for sure. At this stage, I couldn't accuse anyone without

proof. I sank down again, moving as close as I could to the door.

The moment I heard movement coming my way I broke out of my thoughts. I had to get out of there before I was caught. I was afraid to check to see if I could open any of the doors. Any noise would've alerted them. I wanted to kill them both, but I had to be smart. I was alone with no weapons. The power I had couldn't be fully controlled. If it really was Rowan, he could easily make me disappear. I leaped to my feet, scurrying back down the hallway as fast as I could.

After more endless roaming, I found a guard who led me to my room. The evening skies outside my window appeared to be made of purple cotton candy. My body was weak, my empty stomach growled. Before I could find food, I needed to clean up. I slipped off the robe and then unpeeled the bandage on my hand. The injury was fully healed. Whatever those creams were, they must have contained something magical.

Next up is a much needed bath. Afterwards, I'll have to figure out what I can wear to the Ball since my other dress was totally shredded.

Soaking within warm bubbles, I closed my eyes and let the heat warm my aching muscles. My world had been clearer under the poison's influence. Now, I wondered if Rowan was the traitor. If I was correct, who was his accomplice? He didn't seem to have any friends here, especially from his own court. But if it wasn't him, I was sure I'd heard that voice before. His tone was aloof, but terrifying, as if he had no emotion within him. I guessed he was someone with great power.

I had to find out the truth. My next move had to be the right one. For starters, I would attend the council meetings. Based on the conversation I heard, I suspected the traitor would be there. Whether or not it was Rowan remained to be seen. Training with him suddenly seemed more important than ever.

Something told me I would soon be fighting for not only my father's life, but my own.

CHAPTER FIFTEEN

I got up late the next day. It was difficult to fall asleep with the voices I heard behind the door still ringing in my ears. Who were they? One of them had to be part of the air court. It was the only way someone could've gotten close to my father. Someone he trusted. Was it a member of the council? A knight? The possibilities were endless. I rubbed my hands over my face, then I noticed something new sitting at the bottom of my bed.

A plain white gift box.

The poison from the day before must have been in my system a lot longer than I anticipated because I never heard anyone come into my room. I picked up my little surprise for further investigation. There was no note on the outside from the sender. Inside the box, I discovered a canvas colored button-down shirt, a pair of dark jeans, and steel-toed leather boots. It was very urban cowgirl.

I scooted out of bed, trying on my new attire. The loose fitting shirt was thicker than any I owned. I kept a bra and tank top on underneath in case I got too hot. The jeans were skinny cut, which fit my normal style. The boots were just the right size. I wasn't sure why I needed all this, but it was put here for a purpose. I pulled my hair in a ponytail as I headed outside.

Once I got past the archway, I saw Rowan standing

near the entrance to the portal leaning against a tree. My eyebrows furrowed as I took in his new, biker-like attire. Instead of relaxed mortal clothes, he wore black leather pants with a matching jacket and a tight black t-shirt. It was rock-band-meets-the-Matrix, minus the sunglasses. This guy took hotness to a whole new level, but at the same time, something about it made me wonder. Then, a second later, it was clear where my new attire had come from.

I crossed my arms. "Next time you come to my room, I'd prefer you knock first."

"I did." The corner of his mouth curled into a half smile. "You were passed out and snoring like a wild bear."

I wasn't sure if I was angry or mortified. There were a few times I had sleepovers as a kid, but no one ever mentioned me snoring. I had no idea if I really made noises in my sleep or if Rowan was just teasing me. I decided to play it off like I didn't care. "Well whatevs, just stay out of my room."

He made his way toward the enflamed entryway. "You needed flame-resistant clothing for what I have planned for today."

"What exactly do you have planned?" I asked, nerves already building in my belly.

"We're getting to an essential part of your training." He glanced over his shoulder, smirking. "I'm going to get you all hot and bothered."

Heat warmed my cheeks. I was sure they were bright red. Something in his tone made my heart pound harder. Rather than giving him the satisfaction of knowing he got to me, I shook off those feelings, heading through the pathway without saying another word.

We arrived at what had become our spot. Well, it wasn't *our spot* like we were dating and had a special place we called our own. I mean, if we had a spot it would be on the side of the mountain where he finally opened up to me. The beach was where we came to train which was totally different. Then again, the beach was where he almost kissed me—twice. He had pretended like he didn't, but he did.

I was still deep in thought, I didn't notice him standing in front of me with an eyebrow raised, as if he was waiting on me. I seriously needed to snap out of this *thing* I felt for him. He wasn't my type anyway—I didn't even like leather jackets. They were so cliché, but damn did he look good in it. He was all bad boyish with secrets and crazy sword fighting skills and serious family drama from his past. I realized I was doing it again, and I wanted to either crawl under a rock or get the hell out of here. What was going on with me? Why was I thinking about Rowan so much?

It wasn't even twenty-four hours ago that I considered him a suspect. One of the voices did sound very similar to his. Plus he knew Dad and could've easily gotten close to him. Not to mention, Rowan was a warrior. I wasn't sure if he was strong enough to take down Dad, but I was sure he could put up a good fight. Even with all the evidence, I didn't think the voice could have been Rowan. Dad saved his life after all. I don't believe Rowan would hurt him.

I needed to get out of my own head.

Tonight was the Ball and I needed to focus. With Dad still missing, I had to display my elemental power for the air court. I wasn't sure about the specifics, but I knew the fire queen would throw a fireball at me and it was my job to extinguish it. Judging from my only meeting with her, I was sure she wasn't going to make it easy.

"Is it time to start catching some balls or what?" *I did not just say that. Why am I so lame?*

He shook his head. "Don't try to make this sound simple. Trust me, it's not."

I sat on the sandy beach, crossed my legs, and leaned back on my hands. "Okay Master Jedi flame-thrower, show me what I need to know."

Rowan flexed his hand; small flares coated his fingertips. "Do you know what extinguishes fire?"

I had absolutely no idea. I untied my boots, digging my feet into the soft, warm sand. "I must've missed that chemistry lesson. Do tell."

He stared at his hand, fisted, and the flame went out. "Fire cannot exist without oxygen. If you isolate the fire and remove the oxygen, the fire will go out."

Sounded perfectly complicated. "How am I supposed to do that?"

"I've taught you how to push the air away from you. Now, you need to learn to return it into you."

A strange mental picture popped in my head. "You mean, like a vacuum?"

"Exactly."

How was this even possible? It took me days to learn to push the energy out, and now I had only a few hours to learn this new technique. Talk about *Mission: Never Gonna Happen.*

An aching sense of doubt settled on my shoulders. "Why didn't you teach me this first? All that other stuff could've waited until I got comfortable with this. Now what am I supposed to do if I can't figure it out? Let the fire queen burn me to death?"

His face turned serious. "You can't be taught to take in your power without first learning to control it. This is serious shit we're talking about. Anything can happen if you can't maintain your center." He took a few steps away from me, mumbling to himself, then stopped, coming back to where he was originally. "You're going to have to trust me. I did what was best for your safety. Now we're wasting precious time. We need to get started. Are you ready?"

He wasn't wrong. I was wasting time, I had no idea what the steps were in a power training. I rose to a standing position with my hands on my hips. "Let's get to it."

"Find your center like I taught you. Once you're relaxed, think about what it felt like to push the energy out through your arms."

I closed my eyes, taking in a deep breath. A cool breeze came off the ocean as the waves crashed into the beach. The salty air tickled my nostrils. It was easy to see why Rowan brought me here to train. This undisturbed oasis was perfect tranquility.

Power surged beneath my skin, running from my shoulders to my fingers. "I feel it."

I opened my eyes and he was only inches from me. The silver barbell in his eyebrow shimmered in the sunlight. I jolted slightly when his hands cupped my elbows, sending tingles down the back of my arms. Gradually, he backed up while his hands slid down my forearms.

He lightly clasped my wrists, positioning my opened hands toward the sky. "Concentrate on the palms of your hands," he said, his voice soft and seductive. "Envision the energy you feel pulling something toward you, as if you were taking it inside of you." He released my hands, backing up a few feet. An empty ache settled in my chest like I had just given away my favorite book.

Rowan cupped his hands. As he pulled them apart, a perfectly round ball of blue fire rotated in the air. "I want you to position your hands exactly like mine, but don't release the surge of power you feel." I nodded, "Now, concentrate on pulling the energy inside of you while you slowly bring your hands together."

I stared at my hands as they moved toward one another. I felt a suction; my hands were like magnets wanting desperately to join. They smacked together with a pop. I glanced up at Rowan. The fire he held was nothing more than a few strands of simmering smoke. I jumped up and down with excitement. "I did it!" I looked again just to make sure I hadn't imagined it. "I finally made something freakin' work on the first try!"

He winked and my legs turned to Jell-O. "You did great. Unfortunately, Liana isn't going to make it as simple as I did. You have to learn to do that while it's moving."

I rubbed the back of my neck. "You mean while it's being thrown at me."

He cocked his head. "Hence the need for fire resistant clothing."

Yeah, he was right about the clothes, but I couldn't give him too much credit. The guys' ego was big enough. "OK, so maybe you do know what I need," I said, lazily shrugging my shoulders. "Sometimes."

He wiggled his eyebrows. "Leave no doubt, Jelly Bean."

A girl gets caught in her Jelly Belly pajamas just once, and she can never live it down.

But did the nickname really bother me? Maybe not as much as I let him believe. Maybe I was only acting like I cared. Maybe I liked his subtle flirtation. Maybe I wanted him to kiss me—twice. Crap on a cracker! There was no point in denying it anymore.

I had feelings for Rowan.

I spent the next several hours having fireballs thrown at me from various distances. By sunset I was covered in sand and sweat. The good news, I managed to extinguish many of the fireballs. The bad news, I couldn't do it every time and I was weak from all the practice.

"I thought you did really well today. I'm actually impressed." He used the bottom of his t-shirt to wipe sweat off his brow. The curved muscles of his abdomen were on full display.

The urge to reach over and touch them made my fingers tingle. *Look away before he sees you!* "I would appreciate the sentiment more if you didn't sound so surprised."

He paused. I thought for sure he noticed me staring at him. "I ran into Ariel this morning and she told me about the poisoned dress." I wasn't expecting that.

I cringed. "I owe her a serious apology. I said things I should've never said. I even accused her of being involved in Dad's disappearance. I can only hope she'll forgive me."

He shrugged. "She didn't seem to be angry with you when I spoke to her. Mostly, she was concerned about you. I told her you were okay."

"Well, one positive thing did happen during the fitting."

"What?"

"I overheard a conversation in the basement of the castle. A plan, I think. It had something to do with the Ball."

His eyes widened. "And you're just now mentioning this?"

A genuinely valid statement. Why hadn't I told him the minute I first saw him today? *Oh, right, because I thought he was a suspect. Oh, and his new sexy-as-all-hell look that brought on my inability to think clearly.* "Well, I'm not exactly sure of what I heard."

He crossed his arms and with a stern look said, "Tell me everything."

"That's the thing, I'm not exactly sure who it was or what I saw. I was still feeling the effects of the poison when I headed down one of the staircases and ended up in the castle basement. I heard voices coming from a sealed door. I got down on the floor to try to see who it was."

"Who was it?" Blue fire ignited at the tips of his fingers. He realized it quickly, fisted his hands, and the flame extinguished.

The surge of his power made my muscles tense. My body temper rose, which was weird because a cool breeze blew all around us.

"All I could make out were their feet. A man in a nice suit who came off pretty intimidating, and an air court elemental wearing yellow robes. The air court voice I didn't recognize, but the other sounded a bit like you."

He chuckled. "Like me?"

"No, I mean, the door was shut, and it was one of

the thick iron doors. They seemed to be standing in an old prison cell."

"Why would I be meeting with someone in the basement cells?"

"Well, obviously it wasn't you. They were talking about preparations. I came in at the tail-end of the conversation, but it was about everything continuing to go as planned. And they mentioned the council, the Ball, and I think they were also talking about me."

He rubbed the side of his cheek. "Did they mention your Dad?"

"No, but I feel like this air court member was close to Dad. Maybe he was helping the other guy kidnap him."

He waved his arms. "Whoa, whoa, whoa. Whatever you do, don't repeat that to anyone else."

I was overwhelmed with urgency. "Why? I need to go in front of the council and tell them what I saw."

"You saw feet and heard part of a conversation. You can't go to the council until you have solid proof that an air elemental was involved. It could be someone on the council. You don't want to let them know. They could panic and kill your father, Kalin." Rowan put his hand on my shoulder. "You could be on to something, but we need to find evidence before we get anyone else involved."

"But that's what I mean. Nothing's happened. No evidence. No nothing." I took an exaggerated breath. "Something is going to happen at the Ball. I can feel it."

He ran his fingers through his hair. "Kalin, we don't know if they were talking about your Dad. Like you said, they never mentioned him or the kidnapping. You need to be smarter about this. You have to find proof."

"Then help me. Come to the Ball tonight."

He immediately shook his head. "I'll head down into the basement and look for clues while everyone else is at the Ball. This way, no one will get suspicious."

I couldn't help feeling disappointed that he wasn't coming to the Ball. Yeah, it was lame considering the circumstances, but I would bet he looked amazing in a tuxedo. "Okay fine. I'm going to go meet up with Ariel and see what kind of dress I can salvage for the Ball. Track me down if you find any evidence."

He cupped my shoulders with his hands, peering down until we were only inches apart. The cinnamon scent of him was all around and I took in a deep breath. "Try to get this out of your head. All you need to be thinking about is the display of power. Keep your emotions under control. I know you can do this."

So my to-do list consists of the following: Going to the Ball in what's left of my dress, displaying my brand new power by extinguishing a fireball as it's thrown at my head, uncovering evidence to stop a traitor's plot, oh and of course, save my father's life. Sure, no problem.

CHAPTER SIXTEEN

After I got out of the bath, I heard a knock on my bedroom door. When I opened it, Ariel stood there with a gown folded under her arm, a wrapped box in her hand. We made eye contact and the side of her mouth twitched slightly. But when she smiled, the guilt from yesterday churned in my stomach.

I stepped out of the way so she could come inside. She laid the dress and gift box on the bed, then she turned around to face me. She was a total knockout in a beautiful lavender strapless gown with a fitted bodice and flowing empire skirt. Her hair hung down her back in loose curls, and her lips were cherry red.

I held up my hand. "Before you say anything, I need to apologize. I feel awful about what I said and how I left. I was so wrong on every possible level."

The tension she had in her shoulders visibly released. "I'm sorry too. I should have had the fabric inspected. I never imagined something like that would happen."

Ariel had gone out of her way to help me since I'd first arrived. She had become more than just an aid assigned to support me. She was a friend I could be totally honest with. A person who understood me. And no matter what, I did not want to lose her. "You know, I'd rather just forget it ever happened. Are we still friends?"

"Of course!"

I wrapped my arms tight around her neck. It was a hug-it-out moment. "Since we've cleared that up, what goodies have you brought me?"

I released her from my embrace. She held up the dress. To my complete shock, it was the poisoned dress. "How is this possible? Is it safe?"

"Of course! The woodland faeries have their own brand of concoctions. They used some kind of herbal powder to remove the toxins. Then they repaired the damages." She fluffed the bottom of the gown. "I told you, they're the best."

I took a closer look at the fabric. It was perfect. "I'm completely impressed." I ran my fingers over the elegant cloth. It was still as soft as it was on the spool.

Ariel laid the garment back down on the bed. "We've got plenty left to do before you're ready to try it on again."

She spent the next hour twisting and pinning my wavy hair into an over-the-shoulder style. I reached behind, running my hand down a curved braid with tiny flowers tucked inside. My hair was truly glamorous. After my tresses were fit for a red carpet, Ariel applied my make-up. She used subtle cool tones for my eyes and cheeks, but when she got to my lips, she chose the same bright red lipstick she was wearing.

When I saw the finished product, I was overwhelmed. I could not believe it was me in the mirror's reflection. I put my hand on my chest. "Thank you so much for this. Everything is so perfect."

"Not just yet." She wiggled her eyebrows, heading over to the gift box she had sat on my bed, she handed it to me. "Somebody left this outside your door. By the size

of the box, I'm guessing its jewelry. Maybe it's meant for the Ball?"

The only person who had left anything for me was Rowan. Could he have left another gift? Something he wanted me to wear to the Ball? The thought gave me a shimmer of excitement. I opened the box, another soft black box sat inside. It was a ring box. I recognized it from all the engagement advertisements on television.

I opened the box, taking a heavy breath as Ariel gasped. It was a thick white-gold ring with a yellow topaz round stone in the center. The air court symbols were embedded on both sides of the center stone.

I would recognize the ring anywhere.

Dad never took it off.

"What does this mean?" Ariel shrieked.

I held the ring inside my clenched fist. The metal dug into my skin. "It means the people who took my father are here."

Ariel was visibly shaking with what I assumed was fear. Her eyes darted around the room like she expected to find a hidden camera or something. "But how did they get so close to you? And why would they leave the ring?"

Because they wanted me to be afraid, and they succeeded. "I think they want me to know how easy it is to get to me. To make me feel vulnerable."

Ariel rushed to the door. "We need to report this to Jarrod. We have to alert the knights."

She reached for the handle and I put my hand on top of hers. "No. I'm going to go the Ball as scheduled. I won't let them know I've flinched. That's exactly what they want."

"But, Kalin—"

I could not let her go to Jarrod and the knights.

Rowan planned to search the basement for clues. If the knights went searching the castle, they would find Rowan and possibly ruin everything. "You have to trust me here. They won't make a move at the Ball. There will be witnesses everywhere. What I really need to do is to get through the night. We'll deal with this afterwards."

Ariel chewed on her bottom lip. It was easy to see she didn't agree with me, but she had no choice, and she knew it. "I'll stay with you all night. I won't take any chances."

"Come on, girl. I promise, everything will be fine." I let her out the door and followed down the hallway toward the ballroom. I swallowed hard, hoping she didn't notice my anxiety. She needed to think everything would turn out okay. I wanted to believe it too, but I wasn't certain.

Nothing was certain anymore.

CHAPTER SEVENTEEN

The sun set, illuminating the stone hallway with a glint of tangerine. The farther we moved down the corridor, the louder the piano music sounded with a mass of voices in the background. I shook along with Ariel's jitters. Of course, I had no choice since she had my arm wrapped inside hers. At the end of the walkway stood two French style golden doors, both engraved with a mountain landscape etching.

I pulled on her arm, and we stopped. "Come on, Ariel. I need you to be brave with me or I'll never get through this."

She smiled back at me. "You're right, I'm sorry. Nothing has changed. You'll go in there and claim the power for the air court then we'll worry about the rest later."

I wasn't entirely sure who she was trying to reassure. I took the last few steps, settling right in front of the massive door.

Ariel tapped on the door with the leaf shaped knocker. Her arm still nestled in mine, we waited as the door screeched open. The music echoed down the hall while a brush of cool air pushed the curls away from my face. I turned away as the setting sun's light poured out of the entrance. Ariel led us inside, oblivious to the brightness.

I opened my eyes, taking in the packed ballroom. White marble floors sparkled in every direction with couples moving across a crowded dance floor. The women wore exquisite Ball gowns in a riot of colors. All were beautiful—some were made of fabric while others were made of flowers and vines. The men managed to look just as dreamy. All wore black tuxedos with ties, vests, and even some scattered top hats. Each guest had a mask either covering their eyes or their entire faces. Of course, the masks matched to coordinate each couple. It was a scene straight out of Phantom of the Opera.

We stood at the top of a double stairway for several minutes. I was captivated by the orchestra sitting right in between the two staircases. Gnomes from the woodland court held string instruments and flutes, or sat behind various drums. With each hypnotic chord the entire room vibrated in exact unison. The dancers flowed with the music almost like a joint performance. My body stirred with a desire to join them. But before I could take my first step down the long stairwell, I felt a tickle behind my ear.

"Surely you can't expect to attend a masquerade ball without a mask?" Ariel asked rhetorically while she attached the yellow mask behind my ears.

I zipped around, catching a glimpse of my reflection. The mask matched my yellow gown exactly, only covering my eyes and nose. A starburst of diamonds exploded over the middle of the mask, tracing the eye holes. Ariel appeared beside me in the reflection. Her mask had feathers across the top, matching flawlessly to her gleaming lavender gown.

Ariel spun me around until our eyes met. "Now, this part is very important. When the music stops, they will announce you. You'll see your escort on the other end of the stairs. They will say your name and you'll meet him halfway. He'll put your hand inside his arm and you'll walk to the middle of the dance floor. Then, you dance. Got it?"

My heart pounded like a beating drum. "Hold on a second, an *escort*? Why do I need an escort?"

She shook her head, laughing. "Relax, it's only for a few minutes. The escort will help you down the steps. You'll walk, you'll dance, and you're done." She repositioned a few of my curls. "It's no big deal, I promise."

I watched the couples below doing some old-school waltz. The room suddenly felt incredibly hot. A drop of sweat ran down my back and I was sure my face was blood red. "But Ariel, I don't know how to dance like that."

My chest tightened. *Is this what it feels like to hyperventilate?*

She fanned my face with her hand. "All you need to do is concentrate on the music, the steps will come. Don't over-think it."

The steps will just come? Oh good, I'm feeling so much better now!

Ariel's eyes widened for a split second, then she immediately put her hands at her sides and bowed. Over my shoulder I saw the woodland court king and queen. We remained still as they moved toward us. The queen was picture perfect with porcelain skin and long brown hair hanging in loose curls down most of her back. Her dress was a strapless forest green gown with white flowers sewn into the bottom trim. The king looked flawless in a black tuxedo with a green tie matching the queen's gown.

I took Ariel's cue, bowing my head.

The king spoke first. "You've arrived at last, Princess Kalin. The fire and water courts have already been announced."

Now was not the time to tell them about the ring. "I apologize if anyone had to wait. We had a bit of last minute drama to deal with, but it's resolved."

His voice turned sullen. "I had hoped Taron would have surfaced by now. He is an ally to the House of Gheb, as well as the entire woodland court. His disappearance has upset us deeply."

His allegiance to Dad was not a surprise. Dad had told me many stories about his longtime friendship with King Orion.

"I had hoped the same, Your Majesty. I'm sure the council is doing all they can to find him." I lied. No matter how useless they seemed, I needed their help. After the Ball, I planned to call an emergency meeting and tell them about the dream vision of Dad, as well as show them the ring.

The king and queen moved into position at the top of the staircase. "For now, I hope you can enjoy the Ball. The shifting of power is an important moment for your court. Your father would be proud to see you now, Kalin."

I forced a smile. His words sliced into my chest like a sword. King Orion meant well, but thinking of my father in his current state made my heart ache.

The music stopped except for a trumpet drawing everyone's attention toward us. Ariel led me to the side of the steps behind the king and queen, then disappeared into the crowd below. I fanned my hand in front of my face to create a little breeze while I replayed

every step of what Ariel had told me. I hadn't noticed that a man in a black tuxedo now stood parallel to me. Minus the diamonds around the eye holes, he had an identical mask. His hair was slicked back and his face was cleanly shaven. Whoever he was, he had yummy written all over him.

A pudgy gnome in a tuxedo announced, "Presenting the king and queen of the House of Gheb." Rousing applause filled the room as the couple walked down the steps and into the middle of the marble dance floor.

Okay Kalin, this will be over in a minute. Just relax and let him lead you.

The small gnome cleared his throat. "Presenting Princess Kalin of the House of Paralda and her escort." The applause started again and I met my mystery guy in the middle. I locked my arm inside his and he leaned toward my ear. "You clean up nice, Jelly Bean."

Rowan.

The tension in my shoulders relaxed when an all too familiar smirk appeared across his face. Exhilaration bubbled in my stomach. I didn't want to be so excited that he was here, but I was. He led me next to where the woodland king and queen stood. "I thought you weren't coming?" I whispered.

"I wanted to make sure you were safe." He shrugged. "Besides, I look sexy in a tux."

Really, he was hot in everything he wore, but no need to tell him what he already knows. It was amazing that his inflated ego was able to fit through the doors. "You look okay, I guess."

"Just okay?" The music started again and Rowan pulled my body into his. Tingles raced down my spine as his hand tightened around my waist. His other hand cupped mine. "Your flustered cheeks say otherwise."

I rolled my eyes. "I'm hot."

He chuckled. "I'm sure you are."

In the mist of our banter, I hadn't realized we were gliding across the floor like professional dancers. My legs moved as if I had performed this waltz every day. "I can't believe I'm actually doing this."

"I had a feeling you'd be a good dancer."

My eyebrows knitted together. "Why do you say that?"

He was about to say something, then paused. "You have a great partner."

"Partner, teacher, friend. We seem to fit in quite a few categories."

"I don't have friends."

"What about Marcus."

For a brief moment, his lips tightened into a thin line, then returned to his standard serious face. "He's the only one."

The words stung a little. Was everything between us on a co-worker level? Had I read too much into his subtle flirtations? "Okay, then what are we?" I asked, sharply.

He leaned closer to my ear, his breath made me shiver. "Wouldn't you love to know?"

When the last note of the song played, Ariel appeared right next to me. Before I could say another word, I was heading toward the farthest corner of the room. She finally stopped behind a bronze statue of two dancing elementals. I gave her my *what-is-your-drama* look while Ariel peeked around the side of the sculpture.

"Who are you hiding from?" I asked.

"Aiden," she stated, as if I was supposed to already know why.

I tapped her several times on her shoulder until she turned around. "Okay, I'm going to need a bit more information. Spill it."

"He's my betrothed."

"Wait, what?" My eyes widened with shock.

She crossed her arms, staring at the dancing elementals. "His father is a high-ranking knight in the air court, which is why he was chosen. Our union will elevate our family status within the court."

I rubbed the back of my neck. "Okay, this isn't the 1600's. Why is this necessary?"

"Elementals have existed since the beginning of time. The traditions have been around for centuries and they rarely change. It might surprise you to hear this, but most high-ranking elementals have arranged marriages."

I took a peek at the crowded dance floor. A male elemental was scanning the area around us. That had to be Aiden. He had his mask off, revealing high cheekbones and pouty lips. His white-blond hair was pulled back into a low ponytail, he had a very muscular build. For a moment, I wondered what she was really complaining about. He was pretty hot. I curled back around, noticing Ariel's head pointed toward the floor. There had to be something more to her story.

I put my hand on her shoulder. "I'm having a hard time feeling sorry for you while I stare at the sexy-as-all-hell dude searching for you. Am I missing something here?"

She met my gaze with moist eyes. "There is, but it can never happen."

I wiggled my eyebrows. "There's another guy? The plot thickens. Who is this mystery guy?"

"He lives mostly in the mortal world. He's a halfling like you."

Nice to know I wasn't the only halfling around. "I think you should tell your parents. There's no way they would want you to marry Aiden if you're in love with someone else."

"It's not that simple. I cannot refuse an order from the court. If I did, I would be exiled." She leaned to the side, watching Aiden weave through the crowd. "We can never happen."

I bumped her shoulder with my arm. "Regardless, I still think you should try to tell your parents how you feel."

"With my parents, it's only about our social status in the court. Aiden is our best chance for my younger brothers to join the knights. The union makes sense on paper." She wiped away a tear with the back of her hand. "There's no getting out of this. Eventually, I will have to marry Aiden."

I tucked a few of her stray hairs behind her ear. "We'll find a way out of this Ariel, I promise." I winked. "Let's not forget I'm kind of a big deal around here."

She ran her fingers under her eyelids, wiped her smeared make-up and giggled. "Oh, I must look like a total disaster. I'm going to go clean myself up." She hesitated for a moment. "Will you be okay by yourself for a minute?"

"She'll be fine." A male voice interrupted. "I'll make sure she's safe." I turned and Jarrod was standing behind us holding two filled wine glasses. "You both look like you could use a drink."

"You couldn't have come at a better time." Ariel smiled, snatching one of the glasses and chugged it in one gulp.

I was a bit more hesitant. "What's in it? I haven't had the best experience with wine around here."

"It's mortal wine from Tuscany, I believe."

Even though he had been my father's closest confidant, I had to count him as a possible suspect. "Thanks again." I took a small sip of the rose colored beverage. Nothing happened, so I assumed it was okay. "If you'll excuse me, I should go mingle with the other council members. It would be rude otherwise."

"Of course, Princess." He bowed, and Ariel darted for the bathroom.

I made my way toward the dance floor while I thought a bit more about this whole betrothed thing. If most high-ranking elementals have arranged marriages, does that include half- elemental princesses from the air court? My anxiety soared. I was about to chase after Ariel for clarification when a single guitarist began to play. The lights dimmed until the entire room was lit only by pink candlelight. A drummer joined the guitar rhythm. It was hypnotizing. The mass of dancers swayed slowly along with the thumping beat. Following the seductive sounds, I pushed my way through the crowd, hoping to get closer to the orchestra.

Without much thought, I finished my wine, setting the glass on a nearby table. A hand clasped mine. I twisted around discovering Rowan standing there. He stepped back and took a bow in front of me. When he rose, I stared at the shape of his perfect lips. The bottom one was slightly fuller than the top. Totally kissable. Instantly my mouth was dry. I licked my lips.

Elementals circled all around us while we stood— some dancing alone and others partnered in an erotic dance I had never seen. Like never before, I felt a desperate longing for him. A feral desire to crush my body into his, dancing into exhaustion. I reached out for his other hand and several female elementals let out a long, moaning sigh.

Our hands joined and I felt a sizzle at the tips of my fingers. He pulled me into his chest, and with his other hand, gripped dangerously low on my backside. My free hand slithered around his neck, fingers tickling at the bottom of his hairline. With no space left between us, we glided across the dance floor. We spun around in circles, captured by the enchanting song. The tension built the longer we danced. His fingers pressed into my back, letting me know he felt it too. Our motions reduced to barely a sway as his hand skated up and down my exposed spine.

The music came to a stop and we stood still. My arms crossed around his neck. I was desperate to feel his kiss. I traced his lips with the tip of my finger, his body stiffened. His hesitation surprised me. "You're not planning to run away again are you?"

He lowered his head. "You don't understand."

"Then please, explain it to me," I insisted.

Another song had begun, but we stood motionless on the dance floor. He appeared as if he was searching for something to say, but stayed silent.

I stood still, but the room continued to move around me. The dancers around us contorted into impossible positions. I couldn't watch them anymore. Instead, I focused on Rowan. His mouth was moving, but I couldn't comprehend what he was saying. I felt like I was drunk, but how could that be? I had only one glass of wine. Then it all made sense.

Jarrod lied.

He gave me an enchanted elixir.

"Something is wrong," I shouted at Rowan over the music. "Everything is hazy. What I'm seeing doesn't make sense."

He grabbed hold of my shoulders to keep me steady. "Did you drink anything?"

"Jarrod brought me and...and Ariel something," I stuttered. Fear settled in the pit of my stomach. "He said it was mortal wine. He lied."

"I have to get you out of here." Rowan clasped my hand in his, leading me toward the exit.

The music stopped and the sound of trumpets followed. I squinted at the top of the stairway. The fire queen stood ceremoniously in a skintight red dress with her hands clasped behind her.

Oh God, it was time for the power display.

CHAPTER EIGHTEEN

Even with blurred vision, Liana was impossible to miss. Her red dress wrapped snug around her voluptuous curves. Behind her, the three Gabriel Hounds I remembered from the council meeting stood in their mortal form. They each scanned different parts of the room. In their tuxedos, they reminded me of the secret service minus the roach-size earpieces.

I gasped when Jarrod appeared at her side. If the room ever stopped spinning, I planned to grab the nearest sharp object and slit their throats. I had no doubt I was looking at the two people responsible for my father's disappearance. I clenched my fists so hard I broke through the skin of my palm.

Jarrod waved his hands to silence the crowd. It is customary for the king to greet you during these ceremonies, but due to current circumstances, I will stand in his place."

His fake sympathy made me want to vomit. The crowd let out a heavy sigh, and Jarrod lowered his head. Liana put her hand on his shoulder as if comforting him. Rowan was right all along, the fire court couldn't be trusted. Liana had to be the other person involved in my father's disappearance. She could have been disguising her voice when I heard them talking behind the iron door.

Rowan must have noticed my reaction. He put his arm around me, leaning into my ear. "The crowd is eating up his performance. I'm sure the council feels the same. We can't go after him without proof."

Heat raced through my veins like lava. "But *he* gave me the enchanted wine!"

Rowan let out an exaggerated breath. "Yeah, but who gave it to him? He could be innocent in this. Do you still have the glass?"

"No."

He lowered his head. "Then we have nothing."

Great. I had confirmed his guilt and had no way to prove it. The council would never believe me, especially since Liana was a member. Those two appeared pretty chummy up there. I was sure she would come to his defense if he were challenged. I needed solid proof, but how?

My attention returned to Jarrod when he addressed the crowd once more. "Since the beginning of time, we have existed as protectors of the elements. Our four equal powers have provided balance to the Earth's nature, which is capable of immeasurable volatility."

What a pompous ass.

"As the Earth's seasons change, so does control of the elements. We have come here tonight to celebrate the shift of power. As fire wanes, air grows its strength. To symbolize the change, the air court will demonstrate their power over the fire court." Jarrod pointed in my direction. "Princess Kalin, please join us on the center floor."

A drum thumped a slow, rhythmic beat. The crowd separated until a large space opened in the middle of the ballroom. I took a few wobbly steps forward, then Rowan blocked my path. "You can't do this now. You can barely walk in a straight line."

"What choice do I have? Either I follow through, or I relinquish my throne. Without a sibling, the throne goes to the lead knight, which in this case is Jarrod. I would rather burn alive than allow that to happen."

"But, you *can* be burned alive. You're not in the right frame of mind to control your power. You—"

Several elementals around us whispered to one another. I was filled with worry, but completely out of options. "Enough. My mind is made up and you're going to have to deal." I pushed him to the side, concentrating on my steps as I headed toward Liana. She stood about thirty feet in front of me. A blue fireball the size of a basketball floated above her open palms.

I swallowed hard.

This was it.

No turning back now.

I shook my arms at my sides, taking in a deep breath. Ariel stood at the edge of the crowd with her hands wrapped tightly around her waist. She looked like I felt. Okay, I needed to concentrate. Relaxing wasn't an option, but I had to try. I had to find my yellow aura. It was my only chance at not becoming a charcoal grilled Kalin.

Needing a glimpse at my energy, I closed my eyes. My heart jumped into my throat when all I saw was pumpkin orange. *Not good, not freakin' good at all!* I wanted to scream and cry and run away as fast as I could. Using my power when it was out of my control was dangerous, but I refused to hand Jarrod the air court on a silver platter. Dad would die for sure—I would not allow it. I garnered strength from this single thought.

Energy surged from my shoulders to my fingertips. It was stronger than I'd ever felt. Liana's eyes locked with mine—a wolfish grin across her lips.

It all happened so fast I didn't have time to blink.

Like a baseball pitcher, she pulled back and threw the raging inferno right at my head. I positioned my opened palms in front of my face. My eyes squeezed shut. The power released, thrusting outward, and the exertion made me fall to my knees. I peeked through one eye when the crowd cheered.

It worked?

Ariel ran toward me. "You did it! I knew you could."

"I can't believe I really did it." She helped me stand. My legs were about as sturdy as an elephant on a tightrope, but I managed to stay on my feet.

A weight was lifted off my chest. With this challenge out of the way, I could focus solely on finding Dad. For the first time, I was confident. I was able to do this by myself. I—

Beyond the crowd, I saw Liana yelling something I couldn't hear over the noise. Several council members were with her. What was going on? I glanced over at Rowan. Smoke simmered from his two fists.

Oh, no!

He did it.

He put out her flame.

The elementals continued to cheer and congratulate me, but Liana knew it didn't happen. The ceremony didn't count unless I was the one who performed it, right?

But, how? His power should not be strong enough to extinguish a royal flame. None of this made any sense.

Rowan came to my side. "We have to get you out of here."

"What did you do?" I asked.

He took a quick glance around. "Not here."

"Fine, follow me." I tried to walk, tripping over my own feet. He caught me before I nose-dived into the floor. "I think I'm going to need a minute."

"I have a better idea." He swooped me into his arms like some old-school prince charming, carrying me out of the ballroom.

"Dramatic much?"

Rowan raised his pierced eyebrow. "Quit pretending you're not loving every second of this."

As soon as my bedroom door shut behind us, he put me down. I was sturdy on my feet once again. The power drain must have wiped out the effects of the elixir. My room was barely lit. The candles had been snuffed out by the cool breeze wafting from the open window. I closed the curtains. Under the dimmed light, the room held a pinkish hue.

Rowan leaned against the wall with his arms folded in front of him. His silence was another reminder of his secrecy. I went into full interrogation mode. "Tell me what happened back there. And this time, I want the whole truth."

He watched one of the dancing flames flicker across the wall. "What's there to tell? You were about to get killed and I stopped it."

"You shouldn't have. Liana knows I didn't put out that flame. I don't know the severity of the situation yet, but I have no doubt its bad."

Leaning his head back against the wall, he said, "What was I supposed to do? Stand there and watch you roast?"

My anger was blooming. "I had it under control."

He chuckled. "Yeah, sure you did."

I came to stand directly in front of him, making it impossible for him to look anywhere else. "Fine, whatever. We both know *why* you did it. What I want to know is *how*?"

His eyes bore into mine, squinting. "You know how I did it. You've seen me use my powers before."

My magic sparked at the tips of my fingers. "You shouldn't have been able to do what you did. Liana is the most powerful member of the fire court. I don't know much about her court, but I do know her position as queen elevates her power. As a solitary, you should be much weaker, and yet, you extinguished her flame without even blinking."

He stood straight up, closing the rest of the distance between us. Peering down, he said, "What are you asking me?"

No way was I going to let him think he could intimidate me. I leaned in until our faces were barely an inch apart, taking in his cinnamon scent. "I want to know who you really are."

We were in the midst of a staring contest. Silent seconds passed like hours. On the outside, he appeared furious, but there was something else in his eyes. It was almost painful to watch. It was as if he was breaking right in front of me.

Rowan hung his head. "I am the prince who rejected his crown."

I blinked twice to make sure I hadn't imagined what he said. "Prince?" A second later, it came to me. "Is Liana your...mother?"

His tone was grim. "No, she's my aunt. I'm the son of the disgraced queen."

Nothing was making sense, but I had gotten used to that feeling by now. "You said your mother is dead."

He took a few steps away from me, running his hands through his hair, his back was turned toward me. "She was found guilty of treason against the courts and put to death. My brother and sister were exiled for trying to help her escape. Without the protection of the veil, they died a few weeks later."

Something told me the story was about to get even worse. I didn't want to ask, but I needed to know the answer. "Why weren't you exiled with them?"

"Because I was the one who provided the evidence against my mother. And when she tried to escape—" Rowan faced me, his defeated expression made me want to cry. "I killed her."

I had to remind myself to breathe. Now, it all made sense. He wasn't hiding secrets, he was ashamed. He felt responsible for the deaths of his entire family. The cocky exterior was a cover-up for a broken, lonely soul. I tried to get closer to him with a desperate need to comfort him, but he moved farther away with every step I took.

I held my hand out. "Please, Rowan, let me—"

His face reddened with built-up anger. "Let you what? Pity me?"

Tears welled in my eyes. "No, that's not what I—"

"You see? That's why I don't talk about it. I don't need your sympathy. I don't need anyone or anything."

A lump swelled in my throat. "Rowan, please. That's not—"

I jolted when my bedroom door slammed shut.

Rowan was gone.

CHAPTER NINETEEN

I spent the rest of the night tossing and turning. As soon as the sun rose, I changed into my white tank top and jeans, then headed outside. Hours passed as I leaned against a large elm tree on the side of the mountain. The clouds around the castle were puffy, but the sun found a way to shine through, keeping the temperature pleasantly warm.

Three questions were toiling away in my head: How do I prove Jarrod was involved in Dad's disappearance? How can I prove he was working with Liana? And where do things stand with Rowan?

The first two questions would take time to mull over. I thought I could find Rowan and tell him I didn't pity him. I thought he was brave to do what he did, and if he wouldn't have left abruptly, I could have told him. I checked every place that we had ever been together, but nothing. No one had seen him anywhere in the castle since yesterday. Wherever he was, he didn't want to be found. Each time I blinked, I returned to the moment when our eyes met and I caught a glimpse of the utter despair he must have felt reliving his painful memories.

"You know, you're not an easy princess to find," Ariel said, jolting me out of my thoughts. "What happened last night?"

Where could I even begin? Was I supposed to tell

her Jarrod drugged me? Or that Rowan completed my power display? Maybe I should've skipped over the Ball all together and gone right to the part where he told me he was the former prince of the fire court? The more I thought about it, telling her anything didn't feel right—not without proof against Jarrod. "Rowan took me back to my room. I wasn't feeling well."

Ariel waited a few seconds before she spoke, as if she was choosing her next words carefully. "I know it's none of my business, but what's going on with you two?"

I wish I knew. Was there any point in trying to clarify our relationship to her if I couldn't explain it to myself? "Nothing really. He promised to help me train, and that's pretty much it. Why?"

She bit her lip. "I don't know. I just think you should be careful."

Those were not the words I was expecting. "Why should I be careful? Is there something you're not saying?"

"I'm sure someone's told you about his family, right?" I nodded, assuming she was talking about his mother's death. "After the smoke settled, your father offered him a position as a knight. It would never be official because you can't switch your elemental power, but he would have been given every other privilege of our court."

Rowan said Dad gave him asylum in the air court, but never mentioned he'd been offered knighthood. "He did tell me." *Part of the story, at least.*

Ariel crossed her arms. "And you don't find that strange?"

Of course I did. He had no one else. Nowhere to go. Why would he turn down Dad's offer? "I don't know him

well enough to know why he said no, but still, I don't understand your concern."

She ran her hand across the back of her neck. "Think about it for a minute. If he turned down your father's protection, doesn't that make you wonder which side he's really on?"

"I hadn't even thought—"

"Princess Kalin." Two male guards in traditional yellow court ropes were heading in our direction. "The council has called an emergency meeting. Your presence has been requested."

Hope bloomed in my chest. "Do they have news about my father?"

They glanced at each other, saying something I couldn't make out. The younger looking one responded. "We were told nothing other than to escort you to the meeting."

The fact that they seemed hesitant to answer made me wonder if Liana had told them about the botched power display. It didn't matter. I had planned to tell them anyway, although I would have preferred that they hear it from me. I turned back to Ariel. "We'll finish our talk later, I promise."

She smiled from ear to ear. "Of course, please hurry."

The ache in the pit of my stomach felt like a warning. Whatever I was about to walk into was not going to be good.

Just like the last time, I pushed my way through the vines shielding the entrance. As I stepped onto the wooden planks, the sound of rushing river water plummeting over the falls surrounded me. Again, the place was packed with various members of each of the four courts. Most had their backs to me, their attention completely focused on the council members at the opposite end of the room. Each stood, carrying on conversations I couldn't hear.

Liana was very animated with her arms flailing. But when our eyes met, she froze. Each of the other council members seemed to simultaneously realize I was there because they stopped talking. Once they were silent, the crowd parted. There was now a path for me to walk toward the council. An uneasiness crept over me as I took my time through the open walkway. The last time I came to a meeting, they pretended I wasn't even there. This time they were all paying attention, which made me worry that the news was grim.

"I'm assuming you asked me here because you have news about my father." Even though their faces appeared grave, I still held out hope that there might be some good news.

Liana squinted, disgust all over her face. "You were brought here to confess your crimes against the fire court."

Her words seared into my chest like a hot iron. They brought me here to stand trial? This was so *not* how I expected the meeting to play out.

I was about to say something when Jarrod spoke first. "Liana, you have no proof to base such claims." Was he taking my side against Liana? This didn't make any sense at all. What was going on?

Liana turned to face the other council members. "You saw what took place at the ceremony. Kalin conspired with the *deserter* instead of completing the power display. She broke one of our sacred laws and should be punished."

"An exception should be made." A familiar voice called out. The crowd turned as Rowan made his way toward the council. Relief spilled over my shoulders knowing he was all right. I smiled at him, but he never made eye contact. Instead, he was completely focused on Liana. "Her father is missing and she had only days to master her power."

"Ah, yes, her missing father." A wicked grin grew across Liana's face. "A powerful king goes missing and no one can find him." She said, sarcastically.

"Get to your point before I accuse *you* of treason." Jarrod said, his fists balled at his sides.

His reaction continued to shock my system, making me question every conclusion I had reached. If Jarrod had gone along with Liana, and my family was removed from power, he would've been next in line for the throne. Rowan suggested that Jarrod could have been given the enchanted wine without knowing. Could he have been right?

Liana chuckled, clearly not fazed by Jarrod's threats. "Kalin arrived only hours after Taron went missing, claiming she was attacked by a member of the fire court." She points her accusing finger at Rowan. "Coincidentally, saved by the *deserter*."

Rowan reached over his shoulder, releasing his sheathed sword. The crowd moved back several feet while some of the weaker elementals cried out in pain. My own scar burned at the memory of the iron against my skin. "Kalin *was* attacked by a member of the fire court. I watched her attacker burn to ashes minutes after I slit her throat. Only a member of the fire court would ignite into flames after death."

Liana crossed her arms. "Do you have any proof of this, other than the fake necklace you presented to the council? Surely, you can't expect that the council would take you on your word?"

Jarrod headed toward Liana. As he approached, two of her Gabriel Hounds came to stand in front of her, growling in their animal form. The wooden planks beneath our feet rumbled. "For the last time Liana, what is your point?"

This time, she addressed the crowd directly. "I believe Kalin intends to start a war against my court." The room erupted with gasps and whispers. "The false claims were meant to break the peace treaty amongst our courts. I doubt Taron is missing at all. For all we know, *she* killed him for his throne."

Jarrod tried to push through the hounds, but they wouldn't budge. "I suggest you take those words back before *you* break the treaty with *your* accusations."

Enough! My power surged through my fingertips like an electric shock. "I would never hurt my father!" I said, voice coated with anger. The clouds turned dark, thunder rumbled in the sky. "You on the other hand, Liana, are a different story."

Liana faced Rowan with a look of total revulsion on her face. "All of these questionable events point to one conclusion; together they have killed Taron to start a war against the fire court. Once I am dead, our court will be weakened. The deserter will claim the fire court throne for himself."

The room roared with shouting from every direction. Members of the courts argued. Orion, the woodland

court king, came to stand at Jarrod's side. His council quickly circled around him. The water court elementals glanced at one another, but didn't say a word or show any obvious reaction. Likely, they were speaking to each other telepathically, watching passively as the incident played out.

"You're a fool, Liana. I could have claimed the throne without anyone's help." Rowan stood tall and firm. "As Prisma's only biological child, it is my birthright if I so choose."

Fireballs swirled overtop of Liana's open palms. "I would die before I ever allowed it."

Rowan pushed through other elementals until he was directly in front of me in a protective stance. "There's no time like the present."

Liana threw a swirling ball of inferno at Rowan's head. He grabbed it out of the air, extinguishing it in his palm. A moment later, he ran toward her at full speed with his sword raised above his head.

Then it all went to hell.

A battle erupted. Jarrod used his wind power to get through the Gabriel Hounds, but he took a fireball to the chest before he could reach Liana. Fighting broke out all around me. I lost sight of Rowan. Everywhere I turned, members of the fire court were fighting against woodland and air court elementals. Gusts of wind knocked me to the floor while fireballs flew all around. Other elementals drew their iron weapons. Screams of pain rang out, blood sprayed across the wooden planks. The water elementals did nothing more than put out fires which had ignited all over the place.

Two hounds bolted in my direction. I got to my feet a second before a thrust of energy blasted from my fingertips. Both enormous dogs went flying, crashing against two of the council chairs. Neither moved once they hit the ground. I let out a breath I didn't know I was holding. The surge of power left me weak. It was a struggle to stay on my feet.

Rowan burst through the crowd. "We have to get out of here." He put my arm over his shoulders, towing me toward the exit. He sliced through two fire elementals with his sword.

I didn't want to distract him, but I had to know. "What happened to Liana?"

"She escaped."

CHAPTER TWENTY

We returned to the grassy courtyard of the air court castle. Rowan released my arm, a second later he collapsed onto the greenery. Blood circled around an incision on his shoulder blade. Steam rose from the wound. He must have been stabbed with an iron blade.

I fell to my knees at his side, fear racing through my veins. "Oh God, Rowan! What can I do? I still can't control my healing power."

Rowan got to his knees as he tried to stand. I locked my arms under his armpits, hoisting him up. "I have some ointment inside my room."

"I'll go with you," I insisted, whether he wanted me there or not.

He grumbled, but I think he knew he needed help. Either that, or he was too weak to protest.

Once inside the castle, we headed down a set of stairs. When Jarrod said he had given Rowan a room in the castle I never imagined he meant in the basement. He stumbled down the gloomy hallway, lit only by tiny candles inside decayed metal wall sconces. We came to stand in front of a rotted wood door, which Rowan promptly opened.

The room was just as dark and dank as the hallway. The walls were made of gray brick with no windows. The room was barely lit by just a few scattered candles. A

toilet sat next to a small sink at the far end of the room. Slow drips of water tapped against the brown stained basin. The distinct smell of rust circled the room. The only decor missing was iron cell bars. Jarrod had made his feelings known by the lackluster accommodations he'd offered.

Rowan rummaged through the top drawer of a wooden dresser, pulling out a rounded glass container filled with a white substance. He sat on the corner of his small double bed, wincing as he tried to take his shirt off. I sat behind him on the bed. Gripping my hands around the bottom trim of his shirt, I lifted slightly, revealing a cascade of bruises around his shoulder blade and a deep incision. Careful not to touch the wound, I raised the shirt over his head.

A shimmery haze covered his bare back. I edged closer to get a better look. It was a glamour, but what was he trying to hide? Slowly, the glamour faded away and his skin was revealed. I gasped. Even under the shadows of the room, his back resembled something out of a horror movie. I blinked hard, not sure if I was imagining what I was seeing. The tiny white scars I had seen during his workout were revealed to be thicker and brown. Instead of wings, he had two large, blackened scars. His wings had been torn off. The skin around the scars was mutilated, layers overlapped as if they had been sewn haphazardly back together.

My whole body went rigid.

Who would do such a heinous thing?

He curled around, face grimaced from obvious pain. "I can't hold the glamour. The iron...weakened me."

I had reacted so poorly at the sight of his back. It was insensitive and I was embarrassed. "I'm sorry." I had barely touched the tips of my fingers on the top of his shoulder when he flinched. I pulled my hand back.

Conscious of his discomfort, I shifted farther away. "Please," he said, grabbing my wrist. "Can you help me with this ointment?"

Rowan placed the glass container in my hand. I spun the lid open, dabbling some of the contents into my palm. The salve was cold to the touch and as thick as my Jergen's body moisturizer.

"What is this?" I said, putting my hand to my nose taking in the clean peppermint scent.

"It's a mixture of salt, aloe, and grounded-down herbs from the woodland faeries. It will clean out the wound and remove any iron residue. Afterwards, I should heal quickly."

I examined his body. He was covered with cuts, dried blood, and bruises. I was responsible for his pain. He had been at my side since the moment we met. Defending me, training me, watching over for me. Without him, I'd probably be dead right now. My heart broke to see him like this. "Does it go directly inside or around the outside of the wounds?"

"Both."

My fingers trembled as I carefully applied the cream with the tip of my index finger. He growled, but stayed in position. I glanced at his face every couple of seconds. Each time he was watching me intently. His stare sent my pulse racing.

I needed to say something. Anything to get his mind off of the pain.

"What's the story with the scars?" The words came out so casually, even I was surprised. *Subtle Kalin, real subtle.*

His lips pressed together. I didn't think he was going to answer. "I think I'm done with the cream. Do you have anything I can use as a bandage?"

Rowan held out his hand, I gave him the container of ointment. I was surprised when he got to his feet without any trouble. Whatever this salve was, it seemed to work at lightning speed. He opened the drawer, placing the ointment inside. "The scars were a punishment from my mother," he said, in an emotionless tone. "I refused one of her commands."

Stunned by his response—but equally shocked that he answered me at all—I desperately wanted to know more. I pointed to my own back. "Your mother did—"

Still rustling through the drawer, he pulled out several other jars. As he appeared to be reading the side of the container, he said, "No, she ordered my best friend to do it."

I shook my head in disbelief. "But those look like claw marks?"

"Marcus is a Gabriel Hound," he said, bluntly.

I clasped my hand over my mouth. "How could she do that to her own son?"

Rowan found the ointment, bandages, and some tape. He sat back on the bed. "She would never allow leniency in her court. I disobeyed an order and I had to be punished." He pointed to several brown slash marks stretching across his ribcage. "My mother could control the Gabriel Hounds. She forced Marcus to tear off my wings."

I went numb. "How did you survive that?"

"Marcus carried me to this castle. Taron healed me, but as you can see, there was only so much he could do."

Rowan rubbed the new green ointment across the cuts on his ribs. He tried to hide the strain as he applied the dressing but flinched each time. After watching him struggle to hold the bandage in place while he peeled the tape, I took the adhesive out of his hand. He sat somberly as I sealed the tape over the bandages. My fingers ran across his skin. Goosebumps surfaced on the tops of my forearms. Despite the sweat, dirt, and blood on his skin, there was still a hint of his natural cinnamon scent. Even covered in muck, he remained the hottest thing I had ever seen. The perfect contradiction.

Catching myself mid-swoon, I refocused on my task and managed to finish dressing the wounds. When I was done, Rowan maneuvered toward my corner of the bed. We sat next to each other in identical positions until he leaned backwards, balancing on his elbows. I was entranced, watching the candlelight dance across the muscles in his stomach.

He snickered, I assumed he caught me checking him out. My cheeks instantly burned. "What was the command she gave you?" I blurted, trying to take the attention away from myself. "The one you refused."

He shifted to the side, facing away from me. His bare back was exposed, but he had covered most of his scars with another glamour. They appeared faint once again. "Why does it matter?" his tone, emotionless.

Instead of answering my question, he decided to ask a question of his own. I thought we'd moved past that. Things were going so well, then he put up the brick wall all over again. "It matters because you don't want to tell me." Frustrated, my tone came out with more bark than I intended.

Rowan sat up, leveling our eyes. "It's not important."

"Obviously, it is because you are so adamant on not telling me."

"You." He snarled.

"*You*?" I stood, planting my hands on my hips. "What does that mean?"

He ran his fingers through his hair. "She wanted me to kill *you*. That was her command. Happy now?"

"No I'm not happy. I'm not even in the vicinity of happy! Why would she want you to kill me?"

"She thought you were the next akasha," he said, looking away. "She said she would pass the throne on to me if I killed you before your return to Avalon."

The akasha was an elemental who could control all four elements. As far as I knew, there hadn't been one for at least a century. I was sure none of them had ever been a halfling. Why would she think I was one? And why had my father not told me? My trembling hands dropped to my sides. "Why didn't you do it?"

He rose. "I just couldn't, okay? For once, can't that be enough?"

No way could I stop at this point. "You went against your own mother and nearly died for someone you didn't know. Is it so odd that I would ask you why?"

"What are you getting at?"

"I think there is more to the story. There's something you're not saying."

He smirked. "Like what, Jelly Bean?"

I bit my lip to hold back my grin. He was being flirty, but I couldn't respond to it. If I did, I'd never know what he was trying to hide. "The day you saved me in the woods, you said you were just in the area. If that's true, why did you save me? You didn't know me. Why would you care what happened to a stranger?"

Rowan stared at an empty wall. "I don't care."

Now he refused to make eye contact with me? "Okay. If you don't care, why are you here right now? Why continue to protect me?"

He growled. "Dammit Kalin, what do you want from me?"

I tugged at his arm until he met my stare. "Rowan, the same thing I've been asking for since we first met. I want the truth."

"If that's what you want, then fine. Yes, I knew what she would do if I refused her. And yes, whether or not I thought it was right, I did plan to kill you. There was more at stake beyond your life. I had an entire court to think of. Elementals who deserved freedom."

He had been sent to kill me. My father had to know about this. Did my mother know? Was that why I was protected by his knights? "How long ago was this?"

"You had just turned fifteen."

His words burned into me like hot coals. I remember there was an increase in knights around my birthday. They never left my side, even following me into my classes. I assumed it was because I was getting close to returning to Avalon. Had my parents lied to me? I put my hands behind my back so he wouldn't see them trembling. "How did you know where to find me?"

"The fire court had spies within all the territories. Once I knew where you were, I watched you from the woods behind your house. I was there for a few days."

I swallowed hard. "What changed your mind?"

An incredible sadness radiated off him. His eyes lowered to look at the ground. "I watched you. It was easy to see that you were not an akasha. You were more mortal than any other halfling I had ever known. You were so innocent...and beautiful."

Rowan thought I was beautiful? With everything going on, I shouldn't have focused on that admission. But I couldn't help it.

He lowered his head. "I couldn't hurt you. No matter what my mother would do to me."

I shocked myself when I put my finger under his chin, tipping his head up until our eyes met. "And you kept coming back, didn't you?"

"After my mother's death, I feared my adopted siblings would try to kill you. Staying in the mortal world made sense. I could protect you there."

My hand rested idly on his chest. "Because you do care."

He leaned down, brushing his mouth softly against mine. It was a kiss like I had never experienced. One of those kisses in a movie or a romance novel that never actually happens, and yet here I was, having it happen—to me. Everything else in the world disappeared except the feel of his touch. His hands slinked onto my neck, slowly down my back until they rested firmly above my hips. His fingers tightened around the belt loops of my jeans, and in one swift motion, he pressed our bodies even closer.

I let out a gasp.

He pulled back for a second, staring into my eyes as if he searched for my approval. I stood frozen, my sweaty palms shaking. My lips trembled, parting slightly. And again, he kissed me. This time, his mouth crushed into mine. He was voracious. His tongue poked into my mouth, teasing. The further this went, the more my body ached to keep going. It was intoxicating. When he nibbled on my bottom lip, my legs weakened. I lost my balance.

We fell onto the bed, him on top of me.

Tilting his head, he leaned in until he was right above my collarbone. His hot breath tickled my neck as he kissed his way to my ear. Whispering, he said, "I've wanted to do this for so long."

My heart beat faster with every passing moment. An electric force pulsated through my body, urging me toward him as if he were a magnet. I bit my bottom lip. "Then don't stop."

His body relaxed next to mine as he slid his leg firmly between my thighs. My hands curled, gripping the comforter as if my life depended on it. He watched my expression as his fingers crawled through my hair, behind my ear, and down the side of my neck. My eyes fluttered. His hand curved around the side of my face, and again, he delicately grazed my lips. I pushed my body weight against him until he was lying on his back. I was straddled on top of him.

He moaned.

All of the confusion and tension between us had culminated into this moment. I was energized by desire as he ran his fingers under my shirt, unfastening my bra. And then, without warning, Rowan grabbed hold of my hips and sat me next to him.

No, no, no!

"You don't hear that?" he asked, glancing at the ceiling.

Once I left hot-guy-fantasy-land and actually paid attention, it sounded like a riot of voices echoing through the ceiling. "Whatever it is, it can wait."

Rowan got off the bed, slipping on another shirt. "After what happened at the council meeting, I don't think it can."

I was sure my disappointment showed all over my face, but he was right. "Okay, let's go find out."

He pulled me into his chest, pressing another long, lingering kiss on my lips. A tiny groan escaped from his throat. "On second thought, I'd rather you talk me into ignoring what's going on upstairs."

"Tempting, but I think you're right. We really do need to see what's going on."

"Makes sense to go check it out." His classic smirk appeared. "Besides, you probably need some time to recover."

I rolled my eyes. Rowan sure didn't lack in the confidence department.

Crowds of air court elementals filled the great room and continued into the outdoor courtyard. Rather than the yellow robes I was used to, most wore leather and metal body armor. Iron swords hung from their hips. The swell of voices made it impossible to understand what anyone was actually saying.

I faced Rowan. "What could this be?"

He scanned the room. "If I had to guess, I would say war."

CHAPTER TWENTY-ONE

Nervous energy raced through my veins as I pushed through the masses searching for Jarrod. If Rowan was right, I was sure he planned to attack the fire court. I had to stop this. If they did have my father, I couldn't take the chance that they would kill him if threatened.

I reached the center of the group. Oh, this was beyond bad. Fae from the woodland court wore the same attire as the air elementals. King Orion had told me at the Ball that he would join us if necessary.

Once I made my way outside, I found Jarrod with the woodland king. They stood next to a few men passing out swords and shields to a long line of elementals.

Rowan's hand curled around my bicep. "Think before you go charging over there. We still don't know anything for sure."

The weak and bloodied vision I had of Dad appeared again in my head. I jerked my arm out of his grip. "I can handle myself."

"I know you can," he said, releasing his sword from its sheath. "I'm right behind you."

His words of confidence gave me a ping of ease as I approached Jarrod. "Jarrod, what the hell is all this?" I asked calmly. On the inside, I was in freak-out mode.

Jarrod's eyes widened when he noticed me for the

first time. "I'm relieved to see you, Princess. We searched for you and were concerned that you had been taken." He glanced down at my white tank top covered in blood and dirt. "Have you been injured?"

I still wasn't sure I could trust him. He had defended me at the council meeting, but I couldn't forget that he was the one who handed me the enchanted wine. "No, I'm fine. Rowan brought me back to the castle when the fighting broke out. You still haven't answered my question."

Jarrod took a quick glance at Rowan, but did not offer him any gratitude for keeping me safe. What was the deal with these two? "One of our spies told us King Taron is being held in the fire territory. We're going to attack at sundown."

Something about his words did not sit well. The courts had been at peace for years, so why would we have spies? "Do we have any real proof beyond someone's word? Isn't anyone concerned about the treaty?"

King Orion spoke first. "The treaty is void. Liana brought it on herself when she attacked during the council meeting."

But she went after Rowan. Wasn't he technically still a member of the fire court? How could her actions affect the peace between the courts when it was so clearly between them? No, this wasn't the answer. Dad would never approve. I had to come up with another option and fast. "I don't think we should rush into war. We should call another emergency council meeting and discuss this."

"The council has disbanded," Jarrod said, appearing irritated by my suggestion. "We are out of options."

My stomach churned. Admittedly, I wasn't the biggest fan of the council, but learning they had disbanded did not offer any comfort. "How do we know Liana won't kill my father once she discovers us charging into her territory?"

Jarrod ushered me away from the group. "We've spent a week talking and searching and we've gotten nowhere. This news is all we have to go on. We have to act now."

This had gone south of cray-cray. Liana's motives were questionable, but that didn't justify starting a war without proof. "I'm sorry Jarrod, but I won't gamble on my father's life. I want you to stop this now."

Jarrod grabbed my upper arm, drawing me closer to him like a child about to be scolded. Rowan motioned toward us. I held my hand up, asking him to keep his distance. Snatching my arm away, I asked, "What do you think you're doing?"

"You may be the princess of this court, but your father appointed me the leader of the knights. He trusted me, and now you need to do the same." Jarrod glanced around to see who was watching. "We will attack the fire court at sundown as planned, and if he's alive, I will bring him home."

Jarrod returned to the spot where I found him. I stood there dumbfounded. Rowan came to stand at my side. I tried to think as rationally as possible. These were Jarrod's soldiers. If they were anything like the council, they wouldn't listen to me. I had to go another route. "I can't stop this from happening. They don't know me well enough to go against Jarrod."

Rowan made a growling sound from deep in his throat. "I'll make them listen."

He took a few steps toward Jarrod, I put my hand on his shoulder. "No, the last thing I want is more violence. The only way to stop this war is to find my father."

Powerful thunder rumbled in the skies. I had to keep calm or I'd start another lightning storm. A cold wind rushed against us and I shivered.

Rowan raised an eyebrow. "We need a plan."

I paced back and forth. The men had mostly culminated outside now. There were hundreds of them. I didn't like my chances, but I was pissed off enough to take them all on. "If only Dad could have told me where he was."

"What do you mean, *told you*?" Rowan questioned, standing in my way and stopping me mid-stride. "You spoke to him?"

I had only told Ariel about the dream vision, but she dismissed it as a nightmare. "Dad came to me briefly in a dream a few nights ago."

His face turned red. "Why are you just *now* telling me this?"

I immediately realized what a stupid decision I had made. "Because I wasn't sure I could trust you. You aren't exactly Mister Open Book."

He cringed, stung by my words. A moment later, as if putting up another wall, he was all serious-face. "Tell me everything you remember."

"It all happened so fast. There's no doubt he was abducted. But when I saw him, he was in an empty room. He told me I would be betrayed by elementals I trusted, then he faded away with the vision before he could name the traitors."

Rowan ran his fingers through his hair. "Did you recognize the location?"

Had I actually made things worse by not telling Rowan? I lowered my head. "No."

"Describe it to me," he said.

My memory raced. "It's hard to explain. There was nothing on the walls and no windows. It was a dark room—maybe an abandoned building or something. It was dirty and smelled like something had been recently burned there."

"And that's all you remember?" He took an exaggerated breath. "Any small detail could be important. Please think."

I stayed silent for a minute or two as I replayed every moment of the vision. Then, something clicked. "There was a playing card. Like, from a deck of cards and a couple of plastic poker chips on the floor."

Rowan leaned his head back while rubbing his hands over his face. "I can't believe I never thought of this before."

My eyes widened. "What?"

"Nevin," he said, with a disgusted tone.

My stomach tightened. "Who's Nevin?"

"Liana's half-brother. He was exiled from Avalon even before I was born. He runs a few hotels in Las Vegas."

"*Las Vegas*? How is that possible?"

"He's only half-elemental. His father was an incubus, so he's immortal."

If Dad was in Vegas, it would explain the wrinkles on his face. Without the protection of the veil, Dad will be dead in a matter of weeks. "We have to go. Now."

He shook his head. "Nevin is too dangerous. We need to reunite the council and let them decide."

I was instantly infuriated by his suggestion. "No!

We're talking about my father. There's no way I'm waiting here for them to make a decision. He could be in the mortal world slowly dying."

My voice must have carried because several elementals turned to watch us. Rowan leaned down and whispered, "Kalin, you have no idea what you'd be walking into. Do you know what an incubus can do?"

I had read that an incubus could come into your dreams and suck out your soul, but I had no idea what was myth and what was real. Either way, I had no interest in taking part in any soul-sucking activities. Just thinking about it scared the crap out of me. "Not really."

"Nevin can feed on mortal emotions. His ability to influence makes him deadly to mortals, and since you are a halfling, you are vulnerable. If you touched him—even in the slightest way—you would be under his control. You would want to be near him with a desire like you have never felt before. You would never leave his side, and you would do whatever he asked, even if it meant killing yourself." He shook his head again. "No, I can't take the risk."

Holy Spaceballs! I couldn't believe a creature with so much power could live in the mortal world. I crossed my arms in front of me. "I'm going. I'll go by myself if I have to, so you can help me or not."

He let out a growl. "I will take you, but from this moment on, you listen to everything I say."

I nodded, trying to hide my growing fear.

"I mean it, Kalin. No more questions. No nothing. Got it?"

"Got it."

Rowan waited in the hallway outside my room while

I rummaged through my designer closet. We needed to blend in, so fashionable seemed to be the way to go. I settled on a purple Burberry tank top, leather boots, and a pair of Seven jeans.

When I opened the door, Ariel was talking with Rowan. Her eyes were squinted, fists planted on her hips. Yeah, she was pissed.

"What's going on?" I asked.

Ariel folded her arms over her chest. "There's no way I'm allowing you to leave this castle. It's too dangerous."

Rowan must've filled her in on our plans. "I'm sorry, Ariel, but you can't stop me. The only way I can prevent this war is to find Dad. And if Rowan's right and he's in Vegas, he won't last much longer. He's already aged at least twenty years."

Her eyebrows furrowed. "How do you know?" She paused and thought about it for a second. "Are you referring to the nightmare you had? Kalin—"

"So, she told you about it, and you didn't bother telling me or anyone else? You just dismissed it as a bad dream?" The irritation in his voice was about as loud as a slap in the face.

"Don't blame her," I said. "This was my mistake, but arguing isn't going to resolve anything." I turned my attention back to Ariel. "Now do you understand why I have to go?"

"I won't let you go." I was about to say something, but Ariel held up her hand. "Unless you bring me with you. I can protect you."

Rowan chuckled. "You can?"

Ariel pointed an open hand toward Rowan. A strong gust of air propelled him up against the wall, the sheetrock cracked around the outline of his body. He was unable to move. When she raised her hand, he was thrust at least a foot off the ground. He struggled but couldn't get out of her hold. "That's how. Any more questions?"

"Release me," he insisted.

She closed her fist, and he dropped to the ground. Damn, I didn't know Ariel had a little Buffy in her. I seriously never saw that coming. Then again, I had learned to expect the unexpected.

"Remind me never to piss you off."

CHAPTER TWENTY-TWO

The Nevada air was humid, even with the occasional gust of wind. A subtle reminder of the desert that Vegas was built on. Knowing an incubus fed on mortal emotions helped me understand why Nevin would be attracted to such a location. Vegas was all about indulging in desires—a concept I was sure an incubus highly supported. From the bright flashing lights of the casinos to the award-winning shows offering up beautiful dancers in lavish costumes, the possibilities appeared endless.

As we made our way around, I began to see cracks in the shiny, manicured surface. During our scenic trip down the famous strip, we discovered the Statue of Liberty, Egyptian pyramids, and even the Eiffel Tower. The replicas of the famous destinations gave the city a hollow, empty feel. Much like the glamour of the elementals, the beauty of Vegas was its own illusion. Underneath the surface was a city thriving on the addictions of its patrons. Wandering through the glittery streets, we encountered homeless beggars, drug dealers, and pimps offering up pictures of women who sold sex for a living. They left these residents off the advertisements.

The harsh reality made me sad.

We had been walking for so long my feet throbbed.

Passing by the never ending supply of hotels made it seem impossible that we would ever figure out where Nevin was. Each hotel promised the highest of luxuries, yet each time I pointed to one, Rowan quickly rejected it. He said he had a feeling where Nevin would be, but said nothing else as we strolled down the main streets of the city. I imagined Nevin would be at a five-star hotel with a large casino, mostly catering to high rollers with large wallets. A place with exquisite food and drinks were served by men and women who just recently stepped out of Vogue magazine.

While Rowan ignored us, Ariel and I kept each other company. She pointed out all of the tourist attractions, telling me about the history of the city. Her face was animated while she told stories of mobsters, famous murders, and old Hollywood. Her familiarity with this place led me to assume she grew up here before returning to Avalon.

Rowan stopped unexpectedly and we nearly fell into him. He made a beeline toward a crowd around the largest water fountain I had ever seen. We sorted through the swarm of people until we reached the edge of the water. Jets sprayed the water straight up into the air as speakers started to play a recognizable song I couldn't place.

Ariel sang, "Luck Be a Lady" along with the chorus of the song.

I leaned my head into her ear. "Frank Sinatra?" I guessed.

She nodded, but never took her eyes off of the colorful water as it danced hundreds of feet up, perfectly performing to the lyrics of the song.

As the crowd cheered, Rowan announced, "The Bellagio." Our eyes met. He wore a wolfish grin.

Ariel waved for me to follow her as she headed toward the main entrance of the hotel. The moment we walked into the lobby, my mouth fell open. I gazed up at the high ceilings. A chandelier with thousands of hand blown glass flower blossoms covered most of the space. I was breathless. Other tourists bumped into me while they took pictures, trying to get a better look at the artwork. Although I knew I was being moved around, I never budged while I stared aimlessly at the colorful treasure.

Ariel put her arm through mine. "The sculpture is called, Fiori di Como. It was created by world renowned artist, Dale Chihuly."

"How do you know that?"

She pointed to a wooden stand in the middle of the room with an engraved gold plate that told all about the glass blown sculpture and its creator. I clasped my hands behind me while I leaned into the stand. As I stood silently, reading all about the artist, someone tapped my shoulder. An impatient Rowan stood next to me with his pierced eyebrow raised. "Come on."

He led us down one of the many hallways of the hotel. I peeked over my shoulder and saw Ariel following closely behind. Music played wherever we went in a language I didn't speak. Walking within the identical cream-colored hallways made me dizzy. Each had sparkling marble floors covered by lavish maroon rugs. I wondered how many people got lost every hour in this place. My nerves sparked each time a hotel worker passed by. They wore perfectly assembled outfits matching the hotel's decor. I kept waiting for one to ask where we were going, but instead, each only slowed down to greet us.

I caught a glimpse of a sign that read, Conservatory and Botanical Gardens and an urgency came over me that I couldn't explain. All I knew was that I needed to go in there. I inhaled a long breath. My nostrils filled with the intoxicating floral scents. When I turned around, Ariel smiled excitedly which told me she was thinking the same as I was. Rowan, on the other hand, wore an aggravated expression. I made my best 'sad puppy eyes' expression at Rowan and he grumbled under his breath, but followed me anyway.

Once inside, we strolled through an oasis of abundant trees, exotic flowers and plants. The heavenly sweet scents inundated my senses as we wandered leisurely inside elegant glass gazebos. We strolled over a wooden bridge and stood beside a man-made pond that even a nature loving elemental would appreciate.

When we reached the last row of red tulips, I felt a hand around my bicep. I peered over my shoulder as Rowan said, "We have to keep moving."

"Why," I snapped, but I wasn't sure why I sounded so aggravated. We didn't come here to be tourists. This trip was about rescuing my father. But something about this place made it irresistible. "It's beautiful. I want to stay just a little longer." I crossed my arms, happy to challenge him.

Rowan bent down until he was only inches from my face, making it impossible to look anywhere else. My heart raced. "There's a faint pheromone scent hidden beneath the flowers. It's been a while, but I'm guessing...Nevin," he said, pointing to a hallway at the far end of the Conservatory. "The scent is coming from that direction." Rowan turned his attention to Ariel. "We should track it."

We followed Rowan toward the walkway. As soon as we got away from the flowers, Ariel put her hand over her nose. "I can smell it now. It's awful."

Although I couldn't smell it, there was something unnatural about the way I felt. My emotions were heightened. "You can *smell* Nevin? Sounds a little creepy if you ask me."

Rowan let go of my arm. "Every incubus has a unique pheromone they use to attract mortals. To a mortal, they smell like your favorite scent. To an elemental, it's much more potent, like a pollutant. Once you've had more training, you'll be able to sense it immediately."

The farther we went, the more the corridor lined with mortals. Bells, whistles, and cheers filled the air. It didn't take long to realize where the scent led. The casino? Well, that's actually pretty smart. The mortals are drawn to it as if gambling wasn't enough on its own.

"Wait one second," Ariel interrupted, gesturing around us. "Look around everyone. You're standing inside a five-star hotel." She pointed to our clothes. "We can't go into the casino looking like this. We have to blend in, and right now, we look like a bunch of teenagers. There's no way they'll let us set one foot inside."

She was right. All the commercials for the casinos always had women in lavish dresses and men in suits. "Any ideas on how we can get a clothing upgrade?" I asked.

Ariel perched on her tippy toes, scanning the hallway. "I think I see a restroom down there." She met eyes with Rowan. "Go and change into something suitable. Leave Kalin to me."

Leave Kalin to me? What in the world does she have planned?

"Meet back here in fifteen minutes," he replied.

Ariel ushered me into the ladies bathroom which was just as regal as the rest of the hotel. An apple scent lingered throughout a sitting room filled with plush chairs. A wooden end table in the corner of the room held a rounded globe of red rose buds. The rest of the bathroom had the same creamy marble as the rest of the hotel. I followed Ariel inside one of the much larger handicapped stalls.

She wasted no time using her glamour to alter her yellow dress robes into a tight, black cocktail design with spaghetti straps. Apparently satisfied with herself, she turned her attention to me. She reached out for the rim of my tank top, and I stepped out of her reach. "No way I'm wearing something like that."

"We'll drop the glamour as soon as we find King Taron. But for now..." She twirled around. "Let's have a little fun," she squealed.

I held my hands up in retreat, and she went to work. With the flick of her wrist, my shirt and jeans became the exact same dress she was wearing except the color was emerald green. Stepping out of the stall, I tugged at the bottom of the garment. When I caught a glimpse in the mirror, I had red lips and my hair was styled into long, loose curls. Not believing my eyes, I leaned into the mirror and examined the new make-up and hairstyle. "When this is all over, you definitely need to teach me that trick."

Ariel giggled. "I promise."

Peeking out the bathroom door, Rowan was waiting outside. He leaned against the wall, fiddling with the silver bar in his eyebrow. His wore a black suit and maroon tie. With his hair slicked back, he looked devilishly handsome in a James Bond sort of way.

I did my best not to react when I came into his view. My ankles flinched in my green stilettos, I started to wonder if I was setting myself up for a humiliating fall. I bit my lip waiting for his reaction. For a moment, I fantasized he would see me in all my glamorous getup, take me into his arms and crush his lips into mine.

Rowan stood straight up with eyes widened, but said nothing. I was about to settle into a letdown when I saw him swallow hard. Yeah, he noticed me for sure. Feeling confident, I sashayed to the side so Ariel could step out. She was incredibly beautiful, but he didn't react to her entrance.

Rowan cleared his throat. "Let's go."

The casino followed the same color patterns as the rest of the hotel, except we no longer heard the music throughout the rest of the hallways. The constant clinking of slot machine handles and the tinkling of change in plastic buckets filled the air. Most never took their eyes off the slot machines as we casually made our way inside. We passed masses of patrons around the blackjack, poker, and roulette tables. There was lots of noise and the occasional cheer, but for the most part, we heard sighs from those 'oh-so-close' calls.

We came to stand in front of a closed golden door with two muscular guards in tuxedos blocking our path. I noticed a rounded sign above the door that read, club privé in lower case letters. I leaned to the side of

Rowan's shoulder and whispered, "What are we doing here?"

He spoke in an ominous tone to the guards. "We're guests of Nevin. Will you let him know Rowan is here?"

The brown haired, stoic guard nodded, then went inside the golden door.

He returned and opened the doors to an exquisite room in a contemporary art deco style, complete with interlocking chains hanging from the ceiling. There was a private bar filled with rows of top shelf liquor. We stepped onto the raised floor and saw a group of well-dressed men sitting around a dark wood poker table. A slew of exotic women in tiny dresses stood in the background next to a few men who had to be bodyguards. Most of the suited men at the table were dark-skinned, possibly Arabic, except for the radiant one sitting at the middle of the table.

He looked up from his cards, and his almond shaped hazel eyes instantly enamored me. Even though there was a good distance between us, I could barely see the slightly green tint around his irises. His layered brown hair was spiked and styled toward the middle. Aware of my stare, he smiled in my direction, the palms of my hands began to dampen. A black and purple checkered skinny-tie hung loosely around his neck over a fitted black shirt. His forearms were exposed, showing his sun-ripened skin. When he rose from the chair, I noticed that his black khaki pants fit snug around his hipless waist. He had a lean but still muscular build. An energy radiated around him. His warm aura was evidently soaking into my skin.

Oh yeah, it was the incubus for sure.

Nevin made eye contact with each of the gentlemen

sitting at the table. "I apologize for this interruption, but I must attend to my guests." He snapped his fingers and another man hurried to sit in his seat. "Ronald will take my place until I am able to return." He bowed, walking to where we stood. He met eyes with Rowan. "It's been years, Nephew, let's go catch up somewhere. Please follow me."

Nephew? Duh, Liana's brother.

Nevin led us through a hidden door covered by one of the glass and metal screen partitions. The empty room we entered was the exact copy of club privé. The three of us positioned in a straight line while Nevin checked us out. He stopped in front of me and I took in the musky scent of his skin. I admired the hazel in his eyes as they seemed to churn slowly. The color gradually changed into a golden ring of fire. My limbs felt limp, I was fully relaxed. All I could think about was touching him.

"I don't believe we've met, my lovely." His voice was slow and comforting. "My name is Nevin." He held out his hand for me to shake, I slowly lifted my arm from my side.

Our hands were only inches apart when Rowan stepped in between us, slapping my hand away. Pain shot through my arm. I jolted as if I'd just woken up from a trance.

"Enough with your tricks, Uncle," Rowan growled. "I didn't bring her here for you."

Nevin backed up a few paces, smiling mischievously at me. "Too bad, I do enjoy the redheads."

Ariel came to my side, holding my arms while I tried to catch my breath. Rowan had warned me that he would use no restraint with his seductions, and I guess I underestimated how powerful it would be. In those few moments, he was all I desired. Envisioning the fire I'd seen in his eyes, I wondered how many mortals had died under the weight of his control. Anger replaced desire.

Nevin chuckled as I fumed silently. "Well then Nephew, if you didn't bring me something to play with, what's the purpose of your visit?"

"We need to know if King Taron is being held here," Rowan bluntly stated.

Nevin, not looking at all stunned by our request, found a cushioned leather chair and sat down. "And why would you assume I know where he is?" he replied, coyly.

Rowan huffed under his breath, clearly annoyed by Nevin's answer. "Well for one, you're not denying it. And two, you're not exactly known for following the rules."

He put his hand on his chest as if insulted. "You wound me with your accusations. What would I have to gain from attacking the House of Paralda?"

Images of Dad trapped or imprisoned somewhere rushed into my mind. If he was here, he was slowly dying with every wasted second that Rowan spent going back and forth with Nevin. I pulled my arms loose from Ariel's hold and shortened the distance to where Nevin sat. "Enough with the games already. Is he here or not?"

Nevin's lips curled into a wicked grin. "Very well my lovely, I will take you to him. All I ask for in return is a kiss from you."

I blinked and Rowan was standing directly in front of me. "That request is not anywhere near the vicinity of possible." he said through gritted teeth. "You will not barter with Kalin."

Nevin laughed, not at all intimidated my Rowan's anger. "Why Rowan, you defend the halfling so staunchly. Have you fallen for her? And after all these years, I thought I could no longer be surprised."

He's fallen for me?

Rowan ignored his remarks.

Nevin tapped his index finger against his lips. "Very well Nephew, you've been most entertaining this visit. Come with me, I will take you to him."

Nevin directed us toward a hidden door. We stepped inside, finding ourselves standing in a large secret room. It was empty, minus one single light bulb that hung from a wire in the ceiling. The clicks of two sets of footsteps turned my attention toward the shadowed corner of the room. A woman and man came into view. A cold shiver raced down my spine.

What had we just walked into?

The woman had dark brown hair with piercing evergreen eyes. Her long gown had a slit all the way up to her hip. Her arms were crossed in front, and she peered at Rowan with the same disgust that Liana had at the council meeting.

The man next to her had the identical shade of slick, black hair and deep brown eyes with a prominent nose. He had on a black suit with a white buttoned shirt beneath. His stare bore into Rowan. "Hello, brother."

CHAPTER TWENTY~THREE

"Valac? Selene?" Rowan faced Nevin with rage in his eyes unlike anything I had ever witnessed. "You're supposed to be dead."

"Surprise, surprise," Selene huffed. "Aren't you happy to see us?"

Valac put his hand on Selene's shoulder, which seemed to calm her. "Of course he's not. After all, he is the reason we were sentenced to death."

"You nearly started a war with the air court trying to rescue our mother. *That's* why you were exiled," Rowan said, fury in his tone.

The air had chilled. My stomach tightened as if I could sense something terrible was about to happen. Instead of speaking, my glare raced between the three of them.

"Now Rowan, you're being quite rude. Aren't you going to introduce us to your friends?" Valac stepped toward us and Rowan moved in front, blocking his way.

Valac's voice sounded so familiar. There was a calm confidence in his tone. I was sure I had heard it before.

Rowan released his sword from its sheath, pointing it in Valac's direction daring him to come any closer. "Why are you here, Valac. Perhaps I will bleed the truth out of you."

Selene moved into a protective stance in front of

Valac. "How dare you threaten him! I see you haven't changed at all, Rowan. You're nothing more than the deserter I remember. The one who cost our mother her life!"

This was going bad on an epic level. I froze with my hands over my mouth, everything stilled inside of me.

"Our mother died because she ordered me to kill Kalin. Had I followed her order, it would have started an all-out war between the courts." Rowan snarled.

"Enough of this," Valac ordered to his sister, then returned his attention to Rowan. "We didn't come here for revenge, brother. We came here to ask you to join us."

"Join you?" Rowan questioned.

My blood ran cold as I realized where I had heard his voice before. Valac was the one in the castle basement with the air elemental. I glanced down at his shoes. They were the same pair I remembered. "You! You're the voice I heard in the air castle basement. You're the one who took my father!"

"Is she right? Have you taken Taron?" Rowan roared.

Rowan and Valac stared silently at one another for a few awkward moments. "Yes," Valac finally replied, bluntly. "His disappearance was an essential part of my plan to return to Avalon and reclaim the fire court throne for our family."

Rowan turned his attention to Nevin. "And what part do you play in this? Surely, you didn't help them out of the kindness of your heart."

Nevin slyly grinned. "Definitely not. I offered my services in exchange for my freedom. Once Valac becomes king, I will be allowed to return to Avalon or any other place of my choosing." He chuckled. "How could I refuse his offer?"

Liana wasn't involved at all. Nevin betrayed her because she was the one who exiled him from Avalon. I had to learn the rest of his plan. "Jarrod is ready to lead an army against the fire court. How can that help your cause?"

Rowan spoke first as if he had already worked it out in his head. "The fire court won't last long against the air and woodland courts. Liana will be lucky to survive, but I'm sure there's a plan in place for her to die, leaving the fire court without a leader."

Bile rose into my throat. I scowled at Valac. "You're talking about hundreds, maybe thousands of deaths."

"Collateral damage," Valac replied, completely impassive. "The court has already weakened under Liana's reign. I will return it to its former glory."

I shook my head. "What you are suggesting is senseless."

The clicks of footsteps caught my attention. Several elementals appeared out of the shadows. They had the black-feathered wings of the fire court. Settling behind Valac, each held swords raised as if they were waiting on a command.

"I'm going to ask you once more, brother. Join us." Valac held out his hand. "We'll put the past behind us and rebuild the fire court together."

All my anger and pain bubbled to the surface, and I charged toward them. "What have you done with my father?" I demanded.

Rowan rushed me, grabbing my shoulders and pushing me back several feet. I ended up next to Ariel. She stood stunned by my side. "Be ready to run when I give the signal," he said with desperation in his tone.

"What are you going to do?" I asked.

His eyes bore into mine with a sadness I wasn't expecting. "I'm going to get you both out of here."

Both? He didn't include himself. What's he going to do?

Rowan dropped his sword to his side, making his way toward his siblings. "I will join you on one condition."

Valac laughed. "What's your condition?"

Rowan peered over his shoulder at us for a second, then returned to face Valac. "You let them go."

"No, Rowan! I won't let you," I shrieked. This was all my fault. Rowan didn't want us to come with him because he knew it was dangerous. I forced him to bring me, and now he was sacrificing himself so we could escape.

"Remember what I said, Kalin." In less than a second, Rowan had his blade pointed at Valac's neck. The men behind Valac jolted, but he held out a hand. They didn't move. "Now, go! Run!"

"Don't let them escape!" Valac screamed. His men turned their attention on us.

Ariel tugged at my arm, pulling me backwards, but I couldn't feel anything. I was numb. The only sound I could hear was my own panicked heartbeat. I watched in dismay as everything crumbled in front of my eyes. I wanted to burst into tears, or at the very least, vomit.

This can't be happening!

"Come on, Kalin!" Ariel screamed. "We've got to get out of here!"

Unbearable was the only word I could use to describe the next several minutes. Once we ran out the door, I could no longer see what was happening. I heard swords scraping together and a few pained wails, but I didn't know if one of them was Rowan.

We ran through the crowded casino attracting tons of attention. People must have thought we robbed the place. My legs burned as we continued down the streets of Las Vegas. Ariel glanced over her shoulder a few times to make sure I was still behind her. We didn't stop until we returned to the location of the pathway that brought us here.

As we entered the portal, Rowan's last words echoed in my mind. Each time it repeated, a sharp pain stabbed into my chest. I had always wondered if a heart could actually break. If a pain existed so strong that a heart would simply crumble into pieces. After what I had witnessed, I knew it was not only possible, but it had just happened to mine.

CHAPTER TWENTY-FOUR

Leaves crumbled with each step as we made our way through the collection of trees on the side of the mountain. The sun had begun its descent, allowing only small streaks of light to break through. A soft breeze flowed through the tepid air, pushing stray hairs into my face. I removed the rubber band I kept around my wrist and pulled my hair into a ponytail.

Ariel had remained silent since we returned to Avalon. It was likely she was trying to make sense of the last several hours. Or, maybe she was blaming me for everything. I couldn't fault her if she did. Rowan wanted to go alone because he knew it would be dangerous. Had I let him go, he might've been able to save himself. Thanks to my error in judgment, he was most likely captured—possibly even dead.

I wrapped my arms around my waist, trying to hold myself together. Would they have killed their own brother? If they did, it would be because of my mistakes.

Our glamours had worn off, exposing my tank top, jeans, and boots. In the mortal world, we would have appeared like two regular teenage girls, wandering through the forest together. But that was about as far from the truth as it could get. My mind switched between images of Dad and Rowan. I couldn't think about anything else. How would I ever rescue them?

How could I stop the war or find the traitor? Hundreds of elementals could die today, and their blood would be on my hands.

I rubbed my eyes, wiping away the wetness from under my lids.

When we reached the edge of the forest, the air court castle came into view. The setting sun's rays glistened off the corners, giving it a buttery glow. Piles of air and woodland elementals surrounded the castle. In the distance, several practiced sword fighting while others stood in rows as if waiting on a command. If Jarrod stuck to the plan, they would soon leave for the war against the fire court.

I wanted to march up there and stop the assault on the fire court, but I couldn't. I had no proof that Liana wasn't involved or that Rowan's adopted siblings had returned. If I tried to force Jarrod to cancel the attack, the elementals would follow him believing they were saving their king. From their perspective, I would do the same thing. Plus, I still didn't know who the traitor was. I had a feeling that I would be walking into a trap if I showed up now.

Ariel took another step toward the castle and I stretched my arm out to block her. "We can't go in there. I have a bad feeling, that's what the traitor wants us to do."

There was an urgency in her widened eyes I hadn't seen before. "We're out of options, Kalin. We have to take our chances and try to stop them."

I placed my hands on her shoulders. "They won't believe us. Think about it for a second and ask yourself; what proof do we have?"

She backed up and I dropped my arms to my sides.

Her eyes watered as if she was about to cry. "You're Taron's daughter. You *have* to make them believe you."

I ignored Rowan's gut feeling and I lost everything. And now my *Spidey* senses were tingling. I refused to make the same mistake twice. "I'm sorry Ariel, but I need more time. Everything has happened so quickly and I've barely had enough time to process."

"Then I'll just be forced to go on without you." She glanced out to the elementals in the distance, taking a deep breath. There was a pained expression on her face. "My family is part of that army you see there. I won't gamble with their lives while you try to work this out."

All this time, I had only focused on myself, my family, and whatever Rowan was. I had not once thought about her or her family. If there was an award for worst friend ever, I would be in first place by a landslide. "Ariel, please—"

She wiped away the moisture from her eyes with the back of her hand. "I feel awful about leaving you, but I don't see another choice. I have to try to put a stop to this."

I opened my mouth to say something else, but she had already sprinted halfway to the castle. I wanted to scream her name, but knew it wouldn't stop her. Ariel was trying to protect her family, regardless of the risk. She was brave.

Rowan had sacrificed himself because I didn't listen to him.

Ariel walked into danger because I could not.

My mistakes could have cost my father his life.

I felt hollow, as though I had nothing left inside. As if everything that mattered to me had been lost. So I ran—faster than ever before. Maybe if I ran fast enough,

I could chase their images out of my head. Perhaps outrun time itself so I could go back and prevent all of this.

Fallen branches and twigs scratched against my ankles. I never slowed. My legs burned into exhaustion. I was sure I was bleeding, but I didn't care. I kept running everywhere, anywhere, and in all directions. I had no idea how much time had passed or where I was because it didn't matter anymore.

Nothing mattered.

Eventually, something caught my foot and I tripped. I curled into a ball as I rolled down a rocky hill. Sharp edges tore into the bare skin on my arms and legs on the way down. I screamed while my hands extended out, attempting to latch onto something. Dirt got into my eyes and I had to close them. I peeked out of one eye long enough to watch as I rolled right through a strand of hanging vines. I didn't stop moving until the ground leveled.

The soothing, trickling sound of the cool clear stream filled the air. I opened my eyes. I crawled to the edge, cupped water in my hands and flushed out the muck from my eyes. Once my vision fully returned, I glanced over at a beautiful waterfall cascading gently over a large, rocky cliff. Butterflies circled the branches of the surrounding fruit trees. I was next to patches of picturesque multi-colored flowers adorning the side of the stream. It was one of the most beautiful places I had ever seen. If the Garden of Eden existed, this is what it must have looked like.

I took off my shoes, dipping my feet into the cold stream. Goosebumps peppered my calves as I ran the water over the bleeding cuts on my legs. Each scratch sent a ping of pain through my body.

The water in the center of the stream bubbled rapidly like boiling water. I blinked twice to make sure I wasn't imagining it. Slowly, a woman with white henna tattoos on her face rose from within. Her wet aquamarine hair dripped over her shoulders as she floated in my direction. A strapless dress made of coral pink fish scales tightly wrapped her tiny frame, her fingers gripped a gold trident staff. I recognized her immediately from the council meetings. She was the water court queen: Brita of the House of Necksa.

Our eyes locked, and I heard her voice in my mind.

"I'm impressed, halfling from the House of Paralda. The entrance to my palace is a mystery to most elementals, and yet, you stand before me. Perhaps I underestimated you?"

I rose. "I actually found this place by accident."

"I do not believe in accidents, young halfling. You were drawn here and I sensed your arrival at our gates. I also sense something different about you. Your future is unclear to me; too many possibilities."

I had no direction as I was running through the forest. No planned destination. How could I have found this place without even thinking about it? It didn't make any sense. Then it hit me; only an akasha could tap into each court. Was I the next akasha? No, it couldn't be possible. My powers would've triggered by now if that were true. I shrugged it off. "I would like to ask a question."

"What is it you wish to know?"

"Do you have the ability to enter the dreams of other elementals?"

"If you're asking if I helped your father enter your dreams, the answer is yes."

Anger grew in the pit of my stomach. All this time

she had the ability to help him. She could have contacted him even before I arrived in Avalon and none of this would have ever happened. My fists clenched at my sides. "Why didn't you use your power to find my father?"

A rushing wall of water rose from behind her. With eyes narrowed, she replied, *"You would serve yourself well to remember who you are speaking to with that tone. You will be respectful when addressing your superior."*

This conversation was going bad in a big way. Okay, I needed to calm down and diffuse the situation. "I apologize, Your Majesty. I did not mean to disrespect you."

She huffed, crossing her arms across her chest. The wall of water returned to the peaceful stream. *"The connection requires power on both ends. When I tried to contact Taron, his life energy was too weak. I could have killed him if I went any further."*

Judging from my vision, I knew she was being truthful. "Thank you for protecting him."

Silently, she watched me with curious blue eyes. I had a feeling she was in my head again. *"I sense Taron is not your only concern? You care for the shadow prince, Rowan."*

Hearing his name made my stomach knot like a pretzel. Overwhelming guilt gushed to the surface as I replayed the last image of him fighting his own siblings so we could escape. "Can you sense if Rowan is still alive?"

Brita lowered her head, closing her eyes. *"Yes, but his life force is weak."*

Knowing there was still a chance that I could save him released some of the tension in my shoulders. Unfortunately, I had no idea how I could do it alone.

Would the water queen help me? Jarrod said she abandoned the council. Was foresight one of her gifts? Had she foreseen something she wanted to avoid? Regardless, I doubted she would reveal her secrets to me. "Will you help me save them?"

"I will not put my court in danger." With her eyes opened, her stare bore into me. *"The elements are unstable."* She made her way over to me, placing her index finger on my temple.

In an instant, visions flashed in my mind like someone was flipping television stations. One after the other, I saw forest fires, floods, tornadoes, and earthquakes. I was overtaken by the fear of the mortals running from danger. Were those events real? Was this what happened when the elements were unstable?

"If Liana dies, Rowan must be the one to inherit the House of Djin. Only he will return balance to the court of fire." With each backward step Brita took, she receded farther into the water. Soon, only her head was visible above water. *"You cannot fail, air princess."*

Then, she sunk completely into the water until she was gone.

For the first time, I finally understood the full weight of the situation. This was more than an elemental war I was trying to prevent. I had to stop the elements from destroying the entire world.

A lump settled in my throat.

Who was I kidding? I couldn't do this. I was one person. A half-elemental with powers I didn't know how to use. This was too much for me to handle.

Not sure why, but an image of Mom floated in my mind. She was so brave to leave Avalon and raise me alone. I couldn't wrap my head around the amount of sacrifices I was sure she made for me. There was never another man after Dad. I had no grandparents or aunts or uncles. She was always alone. I would have given anything to have her with me. To have her comfort me as she had my whole life.

A dull ache bloomed in my chest.

I yearned for a time when my life was simple. Back to my childhood when she read me bedtime stories over and over again because she knew that made me happy. I loved the years when we would dress up in matching Halloween costumes. She spent hours sewing them which made them better than anything the other kids bought. Or, when she would let me paint dozens of Easters eggs, even though it was impossible for us to ever eat them all. I laughed out loud picturing the multi-colored mess we made on the kitchen counter.

I missed her and I wished I could be brave like her.

But what was I supposed to do? By now, Jarrod had led the armies into fire court territory. Had Valac known what the war was doing to the elements? Did he understand the entire world was in danger? Maybe he did, but he didn't care because he was blinded by his own desperate need to reclaim the fire court.

Regardless, Valac had to be stopped.

I had to let go of my own fear.

I would not abandon the ones I loved. I refused to sit back and watch the world crumble. No, I would go back and find a way to save them.

I cracked my knuckles while I paced.

There was no stopping this war without my father. I had to convince Valac to take me to him, but I would need help. A plan came together in my mind. It was risky, lots of pieces had to fall into place at the right time, but it was all I had.

I pushed through the hanging vines, racing out of

the beautiful gardens. The way back to the air court castle wasn't clear. I had to stop and start a few times as I got my bearings. Circling around, I realized everything looked the same in every direction.

I was lost.

A loud screech shot out from above my head and I glanced into the tree tops. An oversized yellow-eyed brown owl perched on a branch very close to where I stood. He cocked his head as if staring me down. Was I meant to be his next tasty meal? I swallowed hard. He let out another scream then flew over my head. After landing in the distance, I heard him once more.

I had the strangest feeling he was calling for me to follow him. After my Harry Potter moment settled in, I took off after him. What did I have to lose? My breath was heavy as I zigzagged through the trees, pushing limbs out of my way. Every time I caught up to my flying friend, he flew even farther away. I wanted to slow down and rest, but he wasn't having any of it. If I stopped even for a second, he screeched.

Damn bird had a lot of attitude.

In between heavy pants, I thought of Ariel. Had she remained at the castle with her family? I had to find out because I would need her if my plan was going to work. And if I was really lucky, I might also find some elementals and iron weapons.

After what seemed like hours, the owl led me to the edge of the forest where I had left Ariel. As soon as I could see the castle in the distance, he was gone. My muscles tensed as I made my way toward the castle.

There was not a single elemental in sight.

This did not look good at all.

CHAPTER TWENTY~FIVE

When I entered the grassy courtyard, it was completely empty. The castle seemed oddly quiet, deserted even. A cold chill raced down my spine. Was I already too late? I ran at full speed toward the inner chambers. Once inside, I searched feverishly through every hallway running up and down every stairwell in hopes of finding anyone.

I found no one.

Panting, I called out, "Is there anyone here?" No one answered. The emptied halls made me shudder. Nevertheless, I refused to give up hope that Ariel might still be here. My legs burned, I wanted desperately to collapse, but I had to keep going.

I stopped suddenly. I hadn't checked Dad's royal chambers. I turned around, heading in that direction.

This was the one place in the castle I hadn't gone. My footsteps echoed on the white marble floors. The air was thick, almost as if I was walking inside a cloud. Large windows were cut out of the crystal walls, allowing the sun's rays to illuminate the area with a creamy yellow glow. For a second, I wondered how Mom could have ever left this amazing castle, but I moved past those thoughts, refocusing on my search.

At the end of the lengthy walkway, two air court knights stood guard outside my father's door. Their

faces were expressionless. Seeing me, they crisscrossed their spears—iron, I assumed—blocking the entrance as I approached.

"Who's behind this door?" I asked.

Neither guard responded to my question.

My anger grew and I shouted, "I'm princess of this court, and I demand to see who's behind this door!" I didn't recognize my own voice.

"Ariel is being held by order of Jarrod. She is not to leave this room until they return."

I blinked hard. "What? Why? What's happened?"

"We were given no other information beyond that," he answered bluntly.

I pointed to the door's handle. "Open it already." The guard hesitated. "Guys, seriously, I don't have time for this bureaucratic crap. Open the damn door now!"

They glanced at one another once again, uncrossing their spears. I opened the door. Blinking hard, I did a double take when I stepped inside. The walls were more like moving movie screens, flashing images of nature from different parts of Avalon. A yellow-eyed brown owl perched on a wooden stand stared back at me. It was the same owl who'd led me back to the castle.

Sneaky little thing.

Ariel was sitting on the edge of the biggest bed I had ever seen in my life. It was its own island, made of fluffy white pillows. Her elbows balanced on her knees, her hands covering her face.

"Ariel," I called out in a soft voice, "Are you okay?"

She peeked up. The bottoms of her eyes were stained with black, dried mascara. Leaping up, she opened her arms and I hugged her neck.

"Everything happened so fast." Ariel pulled back, so

we were eye level, but didn't let go. "I tried to tell Jarrod and King Orion about Valac, but they wouldn't listen. Jarrod is convinced that Queen Liana kidnapped your father. Jarrod refused to cancel the attack. When I tried to stop them myself, they locked me in here." A tear fell down her cheek.

I shook my head. "The castle is basically empty, minus a few guards. Jarrod has taken everyone with him for what I'm sure will be a blood bath."

Her eyes widened. "There's no way to stop this, is there?"

I wasn't sure. I could only hope. "We need to find my father."

Ariel paced around the room. "Okay, but how can we do that? I doubt Valac is simply going to hand him over."

"First, we have to get you out of here."

"How will we pull that off?" Ariel's shoulders dropped, she hung her head. "The room has been sealed with magic."

"That certainly complicates things."

She sat back on the bed with her hands tucked under her legs. Staring up at me, she said, "I feel like I should have known. I mean, if I had paid closer attention, maybe King Taron—"

"You can't blame yourself. Neither of us can. All we can do is try to stop this war before anyone gets killed."

Ariel rubbed the back of her neck. "Finding King Taron won't be easy. We should come up with a secondary plan in case we fail. If we only had some kind of evidence linking Valac to your father."

"There's nothing other than our word. Valac was very careful with his tracks. Trust me, the only way we're stopping this is to find my father and have him explain what happened."

"But how can we get him back? We can't take on Valac by ourselves. We have no idea who else could be working with him."

My plan raced through my head. "We don't need to defeat Valac. We only need for him to show us where he's hidden my father. If you can create a pathway, then I will distract them long enough for you to grab my father for a quick escape." I held Ariel by the shoulders. "We have to go back to Vegas."

"Wait, wait, wait." Ariel waved her hands in the air. "You're making this all sound really simple and this is *not* simple."

"Yeah," I replied, shrugging. "But what other options do we have?"

Ariel sighed. "None that I can think of."

"Okay then," I said, sounding a lot more confident than I felt. "First, let's deal with the guards so we can get you out of here."

Ariel crossed her arms. "Have you forgotten about this little issue with the magical seal?"

"Leave that to me."

The plan was in place. At first, the guards refused to disobey Jarrod. However, once I explained that the entire court was in danger, they agreed to help us. One guard was sent to find the other council members and make them aware of what had occurred. No telling whether they would help us, but we had to try. Another guard was sent to find weapons in case this got ugly, as I suspected it would.

A short time later, the guard returned with iron swords and blades, which Ariel hid with a glamour. Next, Ariel insisted that I change my clothes since they were torn and bloody from my fall in the forest. She brought me some air court warrior-wear that looked like something straight out of Game of Thrones. I changed into a leather pleated skirt and thigh-high boots. The corset top matched my skirt with the exception of the breastplate, which was strung with chainmail. Gazing in the mirror, I pulled my hair back into a ponytail wondering how anyone would not start laughing hysterically when they saw me wearing this.

Ariel appeared wearing the same thing, except the expression on her face was fierce and confident. My heart kicked in my chest. I fiddled with a knife I had hidden in my breastplate, hoping she didn't notice my trembling hands. I had no idea if any of this would work. If the plan didn't work, I prayed everyone would get out alive.

As she approached me, I noticed her eyes were the deepest violet I had ever seen. "Are you sure you want to do this?"

No, I didn't want any of this. I was scared out of my mind. My palms were sweaty and I wanted to puke. I thought of the simple mortal life I had with my Mom and wished more than anything that none of this were real. "I have to find my Dad before Valac starts an all-out war."

She nodded.

Ariel put her hand out and a wind tunnel pathway appeared. We joined hands. I let her lead me inside.

Please let this work.

CHAPTER TWENTY-SIX

The pathway opened right in front of the entrance to club privé. Two ladies who must have been in their eighties glanced up from their slot machines and shot us a surprised look.

I nudged Ariel with my elbow. "Impressive. Next time, we should just appear in the fountain out front and really give them a show."

"That wasn't me. I had planned for us to land in the alley behind the hotel." She stared off into space for a second. "If the pathways aren't stable, it's likely the elements are unbalanced. We have to put an end to this war as soon as possible or this will spill into the mortal world."

Brita was correct; the elements were unbalanced. "And the good news keeps rolling in." I gave a weak smile to the old ladies, but a bell went off and they quickly returned their attention to their slots. I turned around, facing the entrance. The guards weren't there. I wiggled the knob—the door was unlocked. "I guess it's time to go say hello."

I stepped inside the private club after her. My mouth fell open. The once luxurious suite now resembled an empty storage space. All of the furniture, game tables, decor, and carpets were gone. The large room was dimly lit, only two white bulbs hung from a wire in the ceiling. An ashy aroma lingered, yet nothing appeared burned.

"The creep factor just went up several notches," I said, my voice echoing.

Ariel raised an eyebrow. "What now?"

I was about to answer when a hidden side door creaked open. My pulse raced. One by one, male and female elementals silently lined the walls of the room until we were completely encircled. Although dressed in casual mortal clothes, they marched in unison like soldiers in the military. I wasn't sure how many there were—maybe twenty. Several of the elementals sported tattoos of the blazing fire court symbol on their necks.

It all made sense. Valac was not only fueling the war against the fire court, but also recruiting other fire elementals—all behind Liana's back—for his planned takeover. This was even bigger than I'd thought, which was only going to make my plan ten times harder. I glanced over at Ariel. I could see beads of sweat popping up on the back of her neck. I clenched my fists, refusing to show fear. The elementals watched us as if they were waiting for a signal to attack.

I crossed my arms to hide my trembling hands.

The crowd parted and I flinched. Valac strolled through with his sister at his side. Selene was intimidating, but it was clear she took her cues from her brother. When I locked eyes with Valac, they both took a few steps to the side. Two soldiers made their way through the crowd with a bloody Rowan in tow. I held back a shrieking scream. Valac pointed at Rowan. They released him, letting his motionless body crumple to the floor with a thump. His eyes were closed, his face bruised, and a line of dried blood stained his cheek.

A lump swelled in my throat and I swallowed hard. It took everything I had not to run to him or to react to seeing him that way. Valac had brought him here to scare me, I refused to give him what he wanted. Just as I was about to look away, Rowan's chest rose and fell. He was still alive. My heart fluttered, but I had to push those feelings aside.

I tore my eyes away from Rowan and glared at Valac. "I've come to offer you a treaty with the air court."

"Kalin, don't do this!" Ariel begged, playing her part well. A few elementals snickered in the audience, but I didn't shift my attention from Valac. "I've come for my father and Rowan. If you let us leave with them, then the air court will be your ally and support your claim to the fire court." I concentrated on keeping my voice calm, making every attempt not to appear frightened, even though my stomach was a twisting ball of nerves.

Valac's face was unreadable. "Very well," he said, gesturing toward the hidden door. "Follow me."

The crowd cleared a path and Valac strolled through with his sister right behind. He agreed too easily, which set off my internal alarms. I didn't trust him, but what choice did I have? I met eyes with Ariel, giving her a just-go-with-it look. We followed them through the entryway.

What I saw next made me feel like my chest had caved in. I could not breathe.

Dad was sitting on his knees with his hands behind his back. His canary yellow court robes were ripped, and his normally immaculate brown hair hung clumpy and dirty in front of his face. An iron collar was locked tightly around his neck with charred, bloody skin encrusted around the edges. The collar prevented him from using his power.

Rage fueled me, triggering my power. My muscles simultaneously tightened. I thought about letting loose right here, but I needed to save my energy. I had no idea what Valac might have planned. "What have you done to him?"

Dad looked up and our eyes met for the first time. I placed my hand over my mouth to hide a gasp. He had spent too much time in the mortal world and was aging rapidly. The young man I was used to calling 'Dad', now appeared to be in his late fifties. Dark wrinkles encircled the bottoms of his eyelids, his skin was ghostly pale. He blinked several times and in a faint voice, he whispered, "Kalin?"

I wanted to cry and run into his arms, just as I had so many times in my dreams. I took a few paces toward him, but stopped dead in my tracks as Jarrod stepped out from behind Dad and held a knife to his neck.

CHAPTER TWENTY-SEVEN

"Not so fast," Jarrod warned.

White-hot anger raged inside of me, surging my power. "I can't believe you! My father trusted you Jarrod, and you betrayed him. How could you?"

"How *could I?*" he chuckled. "Do you really think I'd choose Taron over my own children?"

The force of his words made me take a step backwards. I couldn't have heard him right. "What?"

"Valac and Selene are my children."

I stood completely still, dumbfounded by this revelation. "How...is that even possible?"

"Their mother was a fire elemental—she died during childbirth. When it was clear the twins would be fire elementals, I went straight to Prisma. She raised them and she taught them to use their power."

I wondered if Dad knew anything about this. "None of this explains why you betrayed my father. Why did you attack your own court?"

"It's nothing personal," Valac said before Jarrod could respond. "Taron would have never passed the crown to him. Father only did what he had to."

Of course! Valac promised him the air court if he helped him. How very clever.

Jarrod released Dad, coming to stand next to Valac and Selene. Dad winced once before falling on his side.

Ariel ran to him. Kneeling in front of him, she put his head in her lap. She tried to hide her hands, but I saw her trying to rub the salve she made on the skin around his iron collar. Smoke rose from the metal touching her skin, but she continued even though I was sure the pain was excruciating.

I needed to keep Jarrod, Selene, and Valac's attention on me.

Valac waved his hand in the air and a wall of fire encircled the four of us.

I scanned around my new prison. "Nice display of power. I'm sure Queen Liana would be impressed."

Selene let out a disgusted huff.

"Liana is no queen," Valac said, voice laced with venom. "She's a steward of the fire court."

Seems I found a soft spot. Poking away at him might give Ariel time to heal Dad, or at least get him to a point where she could take him to the portal. I had to keep Valac talking. "She *is* the queen. Your queen, if you want to get into the specifics."

Valac rolled his eyes. "Rowan should never have passed the throne to her."

Rowan had given the throne to Liana? That part I did not know. "Who should he have passed it to? You? Oh, right. You were exiled." I tapped my finger on my bottom lip. "Speaking of exile, how is it you're still alive?"

Valac chuckled. "We never left Avalon. All this time, our father kept us hidden away inside Taron's court."

"Okay, then why not avoid all this drama and just challenge Liana for the throne?" I gripped the knife hidden in my breastplate.

He cocked his head. "Every member of the House of Djin has to be eliminated before the crown could be passed."

"Do we really have to kill Rowan?" Selene asked, cringing as if she was expecting to be hit. "If Liana's dead, couldn't we force him to rescind the throne again?"

Valac narrowed his eyes at Selene. "You would show him mercy, Selene? The one responsible for our mother's death?"

Everything Valac said was a lie. He never wanted Rowan to join with him. He was trying to get to him while he had his guard down. "How could you kill your own brother?" I asked, totally disgusted.

Fire ignited from Valac's fingertips. "The throne belongs to me. I would kill *every* elemental in Avalon if necessary." He clenched his fists, putting out the flames. "With Rowan dead and Liana following soon behind, there is no one left to challenge me."

Sweat trickled down my spine. We heard a noise that sounded like scraping metal. Valac lowered his hand and the firewall dropped to waist level. Without knowing we were watching, Ariel removed the iron collar from Dad's neck. His eyes opened and I had to hold back the tears.

"Destroy her!" Valac yelled.

Guards closed around Ariel and she leaped to her feet into a crouched position. A sword appeared from behind her back. When she reached for it, I could see her palms were badly burned. She winced when she gripped the handle. Without missing a beat, she swung it out in front of her as a warning.

A wild roar came out of nowhere, shaking the floor beneath us. A Gabriel Hound. He raced over, positioning himself in front of Ariel and my father. The hound was protecting them. When two of the guards moved toward them, the hound jumped on top of them. They screamed in pain as he ripped them apart. The other guards didn't stand around watching. They ran for the exit. What I was seeing made no sense at all, but it didn't matter as long as Ariel and Dad were protected.

With the attention on the rogue hound, I figured I had about ten seconds.

This was it.

I had to act.

I pulled the hidden knife out of my breastplate, quickly plunging it into Jarrod's chest. He grimaced in pain, but he managed to hit me with a backhanded slap across the face. I stumbled from the shock of the blow.

Valac came toward me, and before I could register what was happening, he punched me in the stomach, knocking the wind out of me. When I bowed forward, I took a kick to the face and fell to the ground. Blood spattered onto the floor and my vision was spotty.

Jarrod pulled him backwards by the arm. "She's mine."

Valac laughed but he didn't seem as satisfied. He was ready to come back and inflict more damage. "I'm not done with her."

Jarrod put his hand on Valac's shoulder. "I should be the one to kill her. It's *her* family's crown I'm taking after all."

Valac paused, then backed away. "Very well, Father. She's all yours."

Jarrod growled as he slid the blade out of his wound. The knife *clanked* when it hit the ground. "You're going to pay for that, little bitch. I'd planned to kill you quickly, but now, I'll take my time with you."

As he resumed his attack on me, my muscles seized

up. I tried to ignore what was going on and ignite my power, but the pain made it impossible to concentrate. Jarrod kicked the sides of my body over and over again. I curled into a ball, turning away from him, trying to block his assault. My breaths were short, possibly from broken ribs. I tried to protect myself, but it only made his attack more vicious. Now he was stomping on my back and shoulder blades. Wheezing and writhing, my strength lessened by the second.

Jarrod stopped. Apparently worn out and needing a break. He said something to Valac, but I couldn't hear what they were saying over the sounds of my own choking and hacking.

In between heavy breaths, Jarrod asked, "Do you hear that sound?" He looked around as if he was searching for something. "It's the sound of your impending death."

Jarrod turned his back to me to gloat some more. My eyes caught a flicker of light. It was the shimmer of the metal blade. During the attack, my knife had somehow slid only a few feet from where I lay. I concentrated all of my remaining strength on my wind magic, pulling the weapon to me. I moved as fast as I could. I leaped to my feet, plunging the blade into his ribcage. I twisted it to make sure I had pierced his lung, then pulled it back out.

Jarrod fell to his knees, I whispered in his ear, "I guess it wasn't *my* death you heard, asshole!" I pushed him and he landed on his face. Winds swirled around his body at a rapid pace. His skin turned to powder and what was left of him floated into the skies.

"No!" Selene screamed. She motioned like she was about to pounce. Just as I prepared for the attack, the hound growled. The floor shook as he leaped through the firewall, landing on top of her. His jaws clamped around her arm, ripping it out of the socket. She wailed in pain.

"I'm going to kill you!" Valac screamed at me.

We circled one another. I didn't have enough strength to fight him, so I had to get creative. Rowan taught me how to suck the air out of a fireball, I wondered if it would work on another elemental. I grabbed him as he prepared a fireball in his hand. Putting my palm over his mouth, I used my power to suck the oxygen out of his lungs. He leaned forward, gasping for air, and I pushed him onto the floor next to Selene.

I blew another gust of wind as I ran through the wall of fire that Valac had created.

My adrenaline kicked in and I could barely feel the pain of my injuries. Ariel was still fighting some of Valac's guards.

A few lay on the ground as they slowly burned to ash. Damn, she had some serious skills with a sword.

The power inside me was so strong that my fingertips burned. Ariel caught a glimpse of me and leaped out of the way. I closed my eyes, concentrating on the remaining guards. Holding my hands out in front of me, I imagined I was pushing the power out from my shoulders through my hands.

A thrust of energy released, knocking me off my feet.

I opened my eyes.

Black blood ran down the farthest wall. On the ground below, some of Valac's guards appeared to be unconscious while others struggled to stand.

Holy shit, I had smashed them all into the wall!

I tried to get up, but I was weakened by the beating I took and the amount of power I used. Without my power, the pain of the fight returned. My muscles felt bruised just like the time I'd gotten in a car accident with some friends from school.

"Ariel, open the gateway now!" I shouted out with as much energy as I could muster.

The hound appeared at Ariel's side. She held onto Dad's hand as if trying to channel his power to help her. A swirling gust of wind appeared; she'd done it. Surprisingly, Dad stood up. She put his arm over her shoulders and guided him through the portal.

I got to my feet, but my muscles ached so much I wobbled.

I couldn't stop, no matter what. The longer we stayed here, my father continued to age. Most important, both Dad and Rowan needed immediate medical attention. I staggered over to Rowan. The hound sat next to him as if he was preparing to be mounted. There was no time to check to see if Rowan was still breathing. I put Rowan on the hound's back, following close behind as he hauled him toward the portal. Tears of pain streamed down my cheeks, but I willed myself to keep going.

"Rowan, please stay with me."

He didn't move.

Once inside the portal, a cool breeze rustled my hair. I trudged forward with every ounce of strength I had left.

When we reached the other side, I was ready to collapse. The portal brought us to some kind of infirmary, much like the one we had at school. Instead of medical supplies, the cabinets contained glass canisters filled with green and brown herbs. The room was lit by white candles resting on large marble pillars and smelled of vanilla. I struggled to get Rowan off of the hound and onto one of the hospital beds.

Rowan was unmoving, but he was breathing. Within moments, the crisp white sheets were stained with blood and dirt. Every part of my body hurt as if I'd been pulled in every direction all at once. A sheeted curtain opened and Ariel appeared out of the side holding a red stained cloth. Both of her hands were bandaged.

"How is my father?" I asked, trying to hide the panic in my tone.

"King Taron is stable and resting," Ariel said, her eyes scanning Rowan's bloodied body. "I'm more concerned about Rowan right now."

Nerves filled my stomach as I watched his chest rise and fall in short breaths. "Can you help him?" My voice shook. "He hasn't responded at all."

Ariel came over and opened one of his closed eyelids. "He's been poisoned by iron." She made her way across the room, opening the top drawer of a white cabinet. When she came back, she had a syringe and a clear bottle of liquid. She tightened a rubber band around Rowan's arm, and a vein popped up.

"Isn't there anything else we can do for him?"

"Normally, yes, but Taron isn't ready to use the amount of power it would take to heal him and neither are you." In one quick movement, she punctured the rubber cap of the liquid bottle with the tip of the needle. She inserted the medication inside the syringe, and then plunged the needle into his arm. "This will go through his bloodstream and prevent the poison from killing him."

My hands were shaking. "What do we do now?"

Ariel retrieved a glass jar from a cabinet, then sat on the bottom corner of his bed. "*We* treat those injuries of yours."

"No." I glared down at Rowan. "He needs your attention more than I do."

Ariel's eyes widened as she looked me over. "Kalin, you're really hurt. Let me help you."

Rowan's eyes were still closed and his expression was solemn. I put my head on the pillow so his face was only inches from mine. His hair was sweaty and dirty, yet still felt soft between my fingers. Underneath the putrid smell of burned flesh, I took in the faint cinnamon aroma of his skin. "I don't want to move."

She sighed. "You'll help him more by helping yourself."

I sat up and she began applying some kind of salve. It smelled like butterscotch, but it burned as she coated each wound. I winced as she applied it to my face and ribs. I couldn't stop thinking about Rowan. "I just wish I had been able to get there sooner. Maybe if I would've told him about the vision, I could have—"

Ariel squeezed my wrist. "Hey, you did what you thought was best. No one can fault you for that. And, by the way, what you did back there, you were amazing!"

After she finished patching me up, I went over to Dad's bedside. A silver bowl sat on a nearby table, filled with red liquid. Ariel must've cleaned his wounds before we got here. His eyes were still closed, but the coloring had returned to his face.

Ariel said, "It will take some time, but I expect him to recover." She ran the cloth over his cheeks. "Unfortunately, I can do nothing about the aging, although, I think he looks quite distinguished."

I ran my hand across his cheek and kissed his forehead. Knowing he was safe and alive filled some of the emptiness I'd been carrying. Each of his breaths came out slow, but steady. It was comforting to watch. It somehow made the world feel peaceful.

I turned around to say something when I noticed the hound standing by Ariel. She nuzzled against his head and said, "Thank you."

"Do you have any idea why he helped us?" I asked, pointing to the hound.

"Before we left the castle, I asked one of the guards to get a message to him. I told him where I'd be and he came to help."

"But why?"

She smiled at him. "I hope it's because he loves me."

I thought back to what she had said at the Ball. "Wait, the guy you're in love with is a Gabriel Hound? *What*? I really didn't see *that* coming."

And just when I thought the surprises were over, the hound shifted back into his mortal form, which happened to be a completely naked—and very ripped—curly, brown haired Latino guy. I looked away as he searched for some clothing inside the cabinets.

"You can turn around now," he said. He'd found a pair of black drawstring pants. There was a riot of cuts and burns across his chest. One of his wounds was seeping blood—it must've been deep. "I'm Marcus, by the way."

Ariel got right to work on the injuries with some kind of liquid antiseptic. As she cleaned each one, he flinched. "Stay still while I patch you up."

Then something Rowan had said clicked in my head. "You're Rowan's best friend, aren't you? The one who tore off his—"

"Yes, I am." Marcus lowered his head. "It was the worst moment of my life."

I looked at Ariel. "Why didn't you tell me about—?"

"Because of me," Marcus interrupted. "I asked her not to tell anyone about us. I didn't want her parents to find out."

I returned to Rowan. He appeared as if he hadn't moved a muscle. I curled up next to him, careful not to touch his body. I bit my lip when all I wanted to do was scream and cry.

Ariel, as if reading my mind, said, "No matter how bad you think this looks, you saved all of us. They would both be dead by now if it wasn't for you, Kalin."

Then it hit me. All this time, I had been burying my feelings because I had to be strong. Those emotions bubbled into my throat and I could barely breathe. I sat up and tried to pull my knees into my chest and I winced in pain. I definitely had broken ribs. Burying my face in my folded arms, I released the tears I'd been holding back. Ariel sat next to me, placing her arm around my shoulders.

Marcus sat in a chair next to Rowan's bed. He squeezed his hand and said, "I shouldn't have left you, brother. I'm sorry I wasn't there, but I'm here now. I'll never leave you again."

Seconds went by like hours without any response from Rowan. The only sound in the room was the intermittent drops coming from a leaky sink. A cold chill filled the room and I rubbed the pimpled bumps on my arms. Each time I blinked, my eyes felt swollen and burned from the tears. Ariel never said a word, squeezing my shoulder to let me know she was there.

I heard a strained whimper. Marcus waved us

closer. A second later, Rowan twisted onto his side. I crawled up next to him and his eyes opened. Relief immediately spilled over my shoulders. I pushed a few sweaty strands of hair out of his face. Rowan reached up and squeezed my hand.

In a weakened tone, he said, "Can't keep your hands off me, can you?"

Marcus laughed. "Some things never change."

I rolled my eyes. "You're incorrigible!"

Rowan smirked. "And, sexy. Don't forget sexy."

Ariel giggled, patting me on the shoulder. "Since you seem to have this under control, we'll go check on King Taron." She pulled Marcus away.

I turned around and squinted at her but she was already at Dad's bedside.

Rowan winced when he tried to sit up. He took an exaggerated breath, closing his eyes. "I'm fine," he said, but I wasn't sure if he was trying to reassure me or himself.

His normal skin tone had returned, but his body was decorated with dried blood-covered cuts and bluish-purple bruises. "Yeah, that's exactly how I would describe you."

"Whatever Ariel gave me is working. I'll be healed in no time." The corner of his lip curled into a half smile. The type that made my legs feel like wet noodles.

"In all seriousness, I'm just glad you're okay." I swallowed hard. "When I saw you lying on the ground, I—"

"Hey, none of that." Rowan tucked a loose strand of hair behind my ear. "The worst of it is over and we all survived."

Flashing images filled my head; the combined air

and woodland courts, leading an assault against the fire court. I was sure the war had started by now, and Valac was sitting back somewhere waiting for the right moment to initiate his own attack. I had managed to hurt him during the attack, but I seriously doubt he was dead.

"It's far from over."

CHAPTER TWENTY-EIGHT

"Forget it!" Rowan shook his head. "There's no way you're going without me."

Ariel watched silently from Dad's bedside. She had diligently checked his heart rate and breathing every five minutes. He was stable, but he still hadn't woken up yet. Based on his wounds, she guessed it might be hours before he was conscious. His time in the mortal world may have also affected his power to heal.

"I don't have a choice. Ariel must stay here with Dad." I scanned Rowan's body. He was healing rapidly—thanks to Ariel's herbs—but still peppered with deep cuts and bruises. "And, you barely survived the last go around. Marcus and I will go."

Rowan slid his legs over the side of the bed and onto the floor. "There's no way I'm letting you two walk into a warzone without me." I opened my mouth to say something and he held his hand up. "Discussion over, I'm going."

"I think she's right, man. You really do look like shit," Marcus added.

Rowan ignored us as he removed his torn, bloody shirt. Without his glamour, the dark scars on his back were visible, but only for a second because he found a white shirt in one of the drawers.

I didn't know what to say, so I said the most obvious

thing that came to mind. "Rowan, this is too dangerous. We all know you're not one hundred percent."

His sinful blue eyes met mine with a soft intensity. He strolled over, cupping my face in his hands and pressed his mouth against mine. For a few moments, everything around us faded away. Our lips moved in unison. His arms overlapped around my arms and his fingers came to rest around my waist. I wanted to stay here forever. I wished I could be a simple teenage girl, just enjoying a kiss from a guy she liked.

But that wasn't my life now, and it never would be.

"Hello?" Marcus said, interrupting the moment. "We're still here."

I hated pulling away. If Rowan had been disappointed, he didn't say anything. Instead, he silently prepared for battle, part of me was relieved. If I had any remote chance of stopping this war, then I needed as many soldiers as I could gather. Even if Rowan wasn't a hundred percent, he was still one of the most dangerous warriors I'd seen. I had faith he would be able to get us through the battle and find King Orion. My stomach twisted into knots.

No matter how impossible it seemed, I had to convince the woodland king to end this nonsense before the fire court was destroyed.

After we collected as many knights and weapons as we could find, we took a portal to the edge of the fire territory.

The scent of rotting flesh filled the air and I held my hand over my nose and mouth. The dark lands were covered with stone mountains and deep valleys, but no foliage of any kind lived on them. The ground was dry. The skies roared with thunder. Within the gloom, an unusually large cloud of smoke hung over a hill less than a mile away. Screeching metal and pained cries could be heard in the distance.

The knights drew their swords. Marcus shifted into his hound form. My sword trembled in my hand. After all the training I'd gotten from Rowan, why hadn't I asked him to teach me sword fighting? I guess I never imagined I would be standing on a battlefield trying to end an all-out elemental war. If we failed, the elements would remain out of balance. It was only a matter of time before this spilled out into the mortal world. Tiny pearls of sweat formed on my forehead.

We trudged up the hill, I swung the sword a few times to get used to the feel of it. It was heavier than I expected, making a swooping sound each time I slashed the air.

Rowan slipped his hand inside my arm, pulling us closer together. "Regardless of what you see or what happens, I want you to stand behind me. If someone comes at you, use your air magic to keep a distance. I don't want you taking any chances by fighting."

"Are you doubting my mad sword skills?" I joked, trying to hide the fear.

He raised an eyebrow. "There's nothing about you that would surprise me at this point, but I know this can go bad quickly." He entwined our fingers. "Please promise me you'll stay with me."

His concern over the situation didn't help my nerves, but we had no other options. "I promise."

We reached the top of the hill and peered down into

the valley. Judging by the amount of carnage, the battle must have been going on for a while. Shriveled gray bodies burning to ash surrounded the fighting. Elementals from each of the remaining courts slashed and sliced their swords at each other. Some fought in bloody hand-to-hand combat. Smoking fire pits were scattered throughout, creating a fog all around us.

We headed downward.

I kept my eyes on the ground, hopping over puddles of black ooze, abandoned iron weapons, and decomposing bodies. The dead woodland faeries dried at a rapid pace until they turned to piles of dirt and dust.

A few of the fire court elementals at the outer edge of the warfare noticed us heading toward them, they threw two lit torches in our direction. Our group broke up into two parts to avoid the flying flames. We scattered and I stayed close behind Rowan. Others turned around, and suddenly, the battle was right before us. There was no white flag, no time to try to explain why we were here. We ran into the crowd with our swords raised, pushing our way through.

Rowan attacked with fluid motion, like he was performing a deadly dance. Marcus was taking out fire elementals three at a time. I was really happy he was on our side. Out of the corner of my eye, several fire court elementals ran toward me at an incredible speed. My power surged and I pushed them back using my wind magic. I tried to keep them away, but my energy slowly weakened with every thrust of wind. I couldn't keep it up, so I gripped my sword tightly and went into defensive mode.

I had no idea what I was doing, but I had no choice. A fire elemental, double my size, came at me and our swords clashed with a loud scrape. He pushed his bodyweight into me, knocking me backwards. The weight of my armor caused me to lose my balance. I tripped over something on the ground and fell back. He stood over me with his sword raised above his head. I twisted on the ground as I tried to get away, but his foot was pressing into my chest. I was trapped. He smiled and was about to plunge his sword into me when a sword pushed through the middle of his chest. My attacker collapsed at my side.

Rowan stood above me with his hand held out. "I could've sworn I told you to stay behind me," he said, shaking his head.

I stood. "I did, but if you haven't noticed, we're kind of in the middle of a war."

Rowan positioned himself in front of me again as we made our way back to the other air elementals. At some point, some of our air court knights found us and helped to form a circular barrier around me. Aching screams of pain rang out, but my wall of protection blocked most of my view.

The knights in front of me came to a halt, and I bumped into the back of one of them. "What's going on?"

Rowan pointed to a clearing where I saw King Orion surrounded by a group of his own knights. They stood, examining one of the dead bodies. Then, a loud horn sounded. The fighting abruptly ceased. "That means the fire court is retreating. Something's happened."

I ran toward the woodland king and screamed out, "King Orion, I need to speak with you immediately. My father—"

"Will be returned to you shortly," Orion said, pointing to the crumpled body in front of him. The body

was charcoaled. I watched in horror as what was left of Liana burned into ashes at my feet. "The fire queen is dead. We will invade her castle and find Taron."

Bitter cold ran through my veins as if my blood had frozen over.

This had played out exactly as Valac predicted. I came to stand in front of the king with my sword pointing down at my side. "You have no idea what you just did." I snarled. Marcus growled. Orion's knights circled tighter around him. "My father is safe in *our* castle. We rescued him, but not from the fire court. Everything Ariel told you was true. Jarrod was the traitor."

King Orion shook his head in disbelief. "Liana *was* responsible. What you're saying is absolutely impossible."

I didn't expect him to take my word for it. "Send your knights back to your territory. You can come with me and see for yourself."

"Very well, Kalin. The battle has been won regardless." Orion headed in the opposite direction with his knights. Most cheered for a victory they thought they had won.

Dead bodies, in various stages of decomposition, peppered the ground. I leaned over and put my hands on my knees. A minute later, I threw up.

CHAPTER TWENTY-NINE

The woodland king, along with the remaining members of the air court council, stood speechless at my father's bedside. After a while, I walked out into the hallway. Leaning back against the wall, I took a deep breath and exhaled slowly.

"They are going to need some time to figure this out." Rowan's voice was soft, comforting. He leaned against the wall next to me with his arms crossed.

"If this little voyage into crazy-town has taught me anything, it's that I can't count on the council."

He turned, facing me. "Yeah, but Taron is back now. They will figure out their next move soon."

I met his stare. "How?" My voice came out more panicked then I intended. "The water court has abandoned the council, and Liana is dead. Who knows how that will affect the air and woodland courts? Once Valac recovers from his injuries, I'm sure he will make the most of all this."

"What about Selene? Did she survive?"

I thought back to the last time I saw her. "She did, but there's something I think you should know."

"What?"

"While you were passed out, Selene didn't support Valac after he said he planned to kill you. It seemed like she was unaware of that part of his scheme." I shrugged. "It isn't much, but I thought you should know."

His raised his eyebrows as if he was surprised. "Selene has always been the mediator between us, but I've never heard of her going against him. This could be a good thing."

"It could mean nothing if Valac's already in control of the fire court."

"As long as I'm alive, he can't make a claim to the throne."

"Well, that's comforting." I rolled my eyes.

Rowan ran his fingers across my cheekbone, then down my jaw line. "You don't have to worry about me. I can handle myself."

I wanted to have faith in him, but his family had proven to be brutal. We still didn't know how many fire elementals they had on their side. I put my hand over his, staring at him. "But, what do you plan to do?"

Rowan straightened his back. "I plan to do what I should've done from the beginning. I had to protect you, but I also needed to protect my court. None of this would have happened if I had stopped my mother years ago."

In my heart, I already knew the answer, but I wanted to hear him say it. "What does that mean?"

"I'm going to return to my home and reclaim the throne."

Marcus appeared out of nowhere, placing his hand on Rowan's shoulder. "And I'm going with you."

I leaned against the frame of my father's door for several minutes watching him sleep. Eventually, I crept inside and knelt at his bedside. The silver bowl still sat on the nightstand with bloodied water and cloths inside.

The dried blood and dirt on his face and neck were gone, but dark bruises remained. I intertwined my fingers with his, resting my head on top of our joint hands.

With my eyes closed, my mind raced. Knowing I had Dad back gave me some relief, but it wasn't over. With Liana's death, Rowan was the last member of the House of Djin—the only fire elemental with a true claim to the throne. Valac would not rest until he was dead.

Dad sighed and I jerked. With his free hand, he rubbed the side of my cheek. "Oh my sweet girl, this is far from the vision I had of our first meeting. I am so sorry you were faced with such danger."

"Why didn't you tell me the truth? Were you afraid I wouldn't come?"

He winced as he tried to lean onto his elbow. I helped him adjust into a sitting position. I perched on the corner of the bed. Once comfortable, he said, "I thought I was protecting you." He hung his head. "Obviously, that was the wrong choice."

After everything we'd be through, I couldn't be angry with him. I thought about the nights when we walked together in my dreams. Back then, he made everything okay. I yearned for that security. He slipped his arm around me and I let my head sink into his chest. My eyes closed as he ran his fingers through my hair. Concentrating on the warmth of his hands, the rest of my worries melted away.

I sat up. "Dad, can I ask you a question?"

"Of course."

There was one thing that was gnawing in the back of my mind. With all the craziness, I really couldn't consider it until now. "Dad, do you believe I'm the next akasha?"

He jolted as if I had shocked him. "I'm not sure I can answer your question. There are tests we can perform, but nothing is one hundred percent accurate—"

"Prisma tried to have me killed. Why would she have risked a war between our courts if she didn't have some kind of proof?" There was an awkward silence for at least a minute. I squeezed his hand to get his attention. "Please Dad, tell me truth. Do you think I'm the next akasha?"

"Yes I do, Kalin."

Keep reading for a sneak peek of
Book Three: *Fragile Reign*

FRAGILE REIGN:

CHAPTER ONE

Rowan

By the time we reached the brush fire, the blaze had spread over more than a thousand acres. The dry heat and wind kept it growing stronger by the hour. Mortal emergency trucks lined the perimeter while sirens rang out to alert residents to the evacuation. I gazed into the skies when I heard a rumble. A plane flew over, dropping gallons of water over the burning forests.

"Do you have enough left to put it out?" Marcus asked, rubbing the back of his neck.

I wasn't sure. This last week had been a strain on my power. Thanks to the unbalanced elements, we'd been traveling the globe fighting one natural disaster after another. The younger elementals living in the mortal world couldn't keep it up on their own. I had no choice. I had to do what I could. "I guess we're about to find out."

"That doesn't sound very reassuring," he replied.

Hidden behind a glamour, we made our way past the firefighters and emergency workers. My nostrils filled

with the scent of ash and smoke. Heat radiated over my face as we got closer to the flames, but the temperature never bothered us. Fire elementals ran hot most of the time. Unfortunately, my clothes did suffer from the exposure. My jeans were spattered with soot and my leather jacket was burned at both sleeves. It was really a shame. That jacket was one of my favorites.

"What do you suppose caused this?" I asked. "Can you pick up on anything?" In addition to his strength, Marcus had an incredible sense of smell. He could recognize the scents of each of the four kinds of elementals. If one of us caused this fire, he'd know it. I feared one of my kind had ignited the forest as retribution for the woodland court's involvement in the attack on the fire court.

After Liana was killed by Orion and his army, rogue fire elementals waged war with the air and woodland elementals. Their forest and mountain territories within the mortal world had been attacked. Some have taken on air and woodland elementals directly. Losses have been suffered on every side. I've done everything to try to end the war, even being forced to take down members of my own court who refused to stand down. The natural disasters and attacks have kept me away from Avalon— away from Kalin.

"I can't tell in this form," Marcus said, unbuttoning his shirt.

He began to shape-shift into a Gabriel Hound. Since I wasn't into seeing my best friend's junk, I looked away while he undressed. Bones popped, repositioning themselves beneath his growing muscles. He tried to hide the pain, but I heard him wincing a few times. No matter how many times he transformed, it was excruciating. I wished I could help ease his suffering. Marcus snarled and I turned back around. Standing on all fours, he was about the size of a panther on steroids. Coarse black fur now covered his caramel skin. I collected his clothes from the ground, stuffing them into my canvas knapsack.

"We need to find the source of the fire." I said, tipping my chin. "Follow me."

I stretched my hands out on both sides. Using my power, I thrust my energy away from us. A pathway formed, splitting the fire into two. We headed straight through the flames. After about two miles, Marcus stopped. His head arched as he sniffed the air. Then he took off. He had likely picked up a scent. I chased him until he circled around something. He couldn't speak in his hound form, but when his eyes met mine, I knew he'd found what we had feared.

Within the blaze, Marcus discovered an area of forest that had not been damaged. It was an oasis filled with lush green trees and flowering bushes. As I approached, I saw what he had already uncovered. It was the bodies of three faeries from the woodland court. Their skin was charred and blistered, but their remains had not dissolved. Woodland faery corpses did not burn like fire elementals. Their remains melted into the ground, becoming one with the lands they protect. Based on the marks on their skin, it was likely because they had been attacked by an elemental in my court. I bent down next to one of the bodies, setting the knapsack on the ground. The woodland elemental was very young. I would guess she wasn't even a teenager. I ran my hand over her face, closing her eyes. A moment later, she began to liquefy into the earth. Anger burned in my chest. I couldn't understand why fire elementals would kill without reason. These fae were children, most likely unaware of the events in Avalon. I stood, vowing to give the slain creatures justice. I swore I would put an end to this violence.

Since there was nothing more I could do for the victims, I turned back to the blaze. I had to save as much of the forest as possible. I closed my eyes, summoning all energy I could from my core. The power surged deep in my chest. I let it extend into my arms and hands. From my center, a ball of energy formed. I focused all of my power into the orb, urging its growth. Every inch of the expansion weakened me. I could barely stand, sensing my knees were about to buckle. When the sphere equaled the size of the forest, I encased the woodland within the energy dome. I spread my fingers then tightened them into a fist. As I pulled my arms into my body, the ball sucked the oxygen out of the fire. No oxygen, no fire. Sweat poured down my neck and I fought to hold on. Little by little, the blaze grew smaller. My arms got heavier, as if someone was adding weights on top of them. My body swayed. I was so close, just a few more seconds. It was too much.

I had nothing left.

I collapsed.

When I opened my eyes, I wasn't on the ground. Marcus was carrying me on his back with my knapsack swinging from his mouth. As he raced through the burning forest, leaves and twigs crumpled under his massive paws. The ground shook with each step he took. Additional planes flew over with water. Some of the liquid landed on us which felt pretty good. The mortals managed to contain what was left of the fire. It was a

relief, a small victory. Now we could rest and prepare for the next challenge.

I woke up next to a large stream in a thick, wooded area. Oak trees that seemed to stretch into the skies surrounded us. A sweet scent permeated the area coming from nearby berry bushes. None of the foliage had any fire damage. I didn't see a single burnt leaf or blade of grass. Marcus must've carried me for quite a while. My entire body ached, as if I were covered in bruises. It would be several hours before I would return to full power.

He sat on a log, chomping down on what was most likely the last of our food. Each time he shifted, he used a tremendous amount of energy. He needed to eat to regain his strength. I could've filled a semi with the amount of food he had eaten this week.

"How long have I been out?" I asked, checking the knapsack to see if there was any food left. I found a sandwich and took a bite.

Marcus stared into the distance. "A few hours." Before I could say a word, he said, "Don't complain. You needed the rest."

Although we were close in age, he acted as my protector. Had my mother still been in power, he would be my slave. My guardian, expected to give his life for mine if necessary. But I would never accept that. Marcus was the reason I survived my childhood. He was family. My brother. Our friendship had been tested when he was forced to remove my wings, but since he returned to my side we've been closer than ever.

"You look so serious. What are you thinking about?" I had a pretty good guess, but I wanted to be sure.

"Do you think her parents will ever accept me?" he asked, shoulders sunk as if he already knew the answer.

Before we left Avalon, Ariel had gone to her parents and demanded to be let out of her engagement with Aiden. Holding Marcus's hand, she explained she was in love with him. Her parents wanted nothing to do with it. Marcus wasn't an air elemental. Making matters worse, he was still considered a slave in the fire court. Ariel's parents were too obsessed with their own social standings to see how happy their daughter was. They threatened to banish her from the air court. Of course, Kalin would never let that happen.

My chest tightened each time I thought of Kalin. I hadn't seen her in over a week. Each day I worried about her father's recovery. Until he could resume his position as king, she was expected to fill in. This meant she would have to attend air court council meetings in his place. She was the one who went to them to reveal Jarrod was the traitor. Since her father is still recovering, she would have to choose someone to replace him. It's an incredible amount of responsibility for someone so new to the elemental world. Much more than she was expecting, I'm sure.

I sat next to Marcus on top of a log. "Listen, Ariel's parents don't need to accept you. If you love each other, that's all that matters."

He threw a few stones into the stream. "Not to Ariel. She feels responsible for her younger siblings. She thinks she has to marry into a high ranking family so that her brothers can become knights."

I put my hand on his shoulder. "If that's the case,

there's nothing to worry about." Marcus turned to face me. "Kalin is her best friend and the future ruler of the air court. She would knight all of her siblings if it meant Ariel could be with who she wants."

Marcus shook his head, letting out an exaggerated breath. "I don't think it's that simple."

My eyebrows furrowed. "Why not?"

"Ariel said there are powerful council members who don't want to see a halfling ruler."

I let out a low growl. I couldn't believe after everything Kalin had done—everything she had sacrificed—to save her court, there were still elementals who would stand against her. I wished I were there. I would love to set them straight...with my fists. "What a bunch of idiots."

Marcus turned his head sharply. "Do you hear that?"

I listened closely. "Nothing."

He stood, pointing to the left. "It's coming from that direction."

A scream rang out. "I heard that." I unsheathed my sword.

I ran in the direction of the noise. Pained wails got louder the farther we went. I could tell by the sound, it was definitely an elemental in danger—most likely a woodland fae. When the ground shook, I glanced to the side. Marcus had changed into his hound form. He must have been expecting a battle. I hoped whatever rest I had gotten was enough. My power wasn't at full capacity, but I could swing my sword. As long as there weren't too many, we would be all right.

Then we saw the source of the pained cries. Two nasty looking goblins in armor were attacking a tiny tree

elf. The elf used his sand magic to shift away their fireballs, but he wouldn't last long. Marcus let out a howl, knocking all of them off their feet. The elf used our distraction to leap into a nearby pathway. The two goblins tried to run, but they were no match for Marcus. Hounds were the fastest elementals in our court. By the time I reached them, he had both under his paws.

"Since you seem to enjoy picking on small creatures, I thought I'd let my ginormous friend play with *you* for a while." I smirked, patting Marcus on the head. "I do have to warn you, he gets a bit rough."

Marcus bent his head, growling.

Beads of sweat trickled down their faces. "Don't kill us." One begged. "We were only following orders."

"Do you know who I am, creature?" I pressed my boot into one of their wrists, forcing the goblin to release his sword. I wasn't going to take the chance that he might get brave and slice into Marcus.

"Rowan, the deserter." The other goblin said, swallowing hard.

"If you know who I am, then you know what I do to little goblins that don't answer my questions truthfully." They both nodded, appearing too scared to lie. But who would command them to kill members of the woodland court? The fire court currently had no leader. Liana was dead. I needed to know more. I bent, resting my hands on my knees. "I want to know who ordered you to attack the elf."

In unison, they said, "Our future king, Valac."

ACKNOWLEDGMENTS

There have been so many people who have helped me throughout my journey. The first in a long line are my parents, Russell and Brenda Howell. They turned into a publicity team after *The Shadow Prince* was released. If my dad wasn't asking random strangers to download my novella, Mom was handing out print copies. They are the best parents in the world. Seriously, I don't deserve them. I want to send out a special thank you to my husband, Christopher. You have been so patient throughout this process. Thank you for making sure my life didn't fall apart while I was writing and editing. You are full of awesome! Big hugs and kisses to my daughter, Madison. She really liked having her name in the acknowledgments of the novella. I'm sorry I couldn't put your name on the cover of this book as you requested. It just wouldn't fit, babe. A big thank you to Courtney Koschel for all your editing magic. I always enjoy reading your comments, especially the ones where you seem to be speaking directly to my characters. LOL! I can't go without mentioning my family and friends who have been pimping this series. I want you to know I really appreciate your support. Here are the unofficial members of my street team: Michael Howell, Megan DeMarco, Cathy Schoen, John Ballengee, Barb Ballengee, Chuck Ballengee, Bob Latimer, Pam White, Jen Scicchitano, and Jessica Reigle. Thank you to all the

bloggers who have read the novella and helped spread the word over social media. I love you ladies so much! Last, but not least, I want to thank you—the reader. Thank you for giving me a chance. This series has been a labor of love and I truly appreciate your support. Big, awkward virtual hug coming your way. ;-)

ABOUT THE AUTHOR

Stacey O'Neale lives in Annapolis, Maryland. When she's not writing, she spends her time fangirling over books, blogging, watching fantasy television shows, cheering for the Baltimore Ravens, and hanging out with her husband and daughter.

Her career in publishing started as a blogger-turned-publicist for two successful small publishers. Stacey writes young adult paranormal romance and adult science fiction romance. Her books always include swoon-worthy heroes, snarky heroines, and lots of kissing.

Stacey loves hearing from readers. Follow her on Twitter @StaceyONeale, look for her on Facebook, Pinterest, and Goodreads. You can also visit her blog at http://staceyoneale.com/.

Made in the USA
Middletown, DE
23 April 2015